# Late Bloomers

John Nieman

Copyright 2023 by John Nieman

All rights reserved. This book or any portion thereof may not be reproduced or used in any manner whatsoever without the express written permission of the publisher except for the use of brief quotation in a book review.

Inquiries and Book Orders should be addressed to:

Great Writers Media
Email: info@greatwritersmedia.com
Phone: 877-600-5469

ISBN: 979-8-89175-019-7 (sc)
ISBN: 979-8-89175-020-3 (ebk)

For Yvonne

# CONTENTS

# CHAPTER 1

## *Spring Fever*

FOR MANY YEARS NOW, MARCH HAD BEEN one of Margot Roberts' favorite months. For one thing, as a Westchester New Yorker, it generally marked the end of the colder days of winter. You could often see couples romantically walking hand in hand around the block wearing just a light jacket. You could also see teenagers kicking an early soccer ball or walking their Golden Retriever beyond the back yard.

Unfortunately, those were not things that filled Margot's bright afternoons these days. Her dear husband of twenty-one years had passed away five years ago.

It had been a storybook marriage with two successful people who often travelled together and at least a few times a month shared dinners in fancy restaurants.

It was easier to do that when their teenage daughter Annie was still home.

A few years back, the 18-year old got a scholarship at St. Andrew's College in Scotland, where she studied international business and then moved onto Cambridge where she gained a master's degree.

Evidently, the young woman inherited the genes of both her parents. Her dad, George, had been a successful stockbroker at Merrill Lynch for many decades until he suffered a sudden and fatal heart attack.

Margot had also spent her post college years in the financial world. She started as a bank teller for Citibank in Hastings, New York. After several decades rising up the ladder, she became a wealth management advisor, earning more $150.000 a year.

It barely compensated for life alone in Dobbs Ferry, New York. However, there were some bright spots in her early spring days.

On this particular weekend, she played many of the LP's that had been shelved since Christmas. She particularly enjoyed "I can see clearly Now," by Johnny Nash, "April Come She Will, " by Simon & Garfunkel, and "Here Comes the Sun," by Consequently, she ordered some hydrangeas, summer lilies and packs of pansies…which she happily planted on Sunday. She also bought several orchids bouquets, which she placed on the dining room table and on the living room cocktail table.

The entire experience brightened her weekend. By Sunday night, she was smiling, and even looking forward to her Monday morning at Citibank. She brought one of the orchid bouquets to her office desk, and began serving the needs of many clients, most of whom had pre-ordained meeting times.

Her typical customers had financial needs—either emergency-oriented or forward-looking. The emergency-oriented could vary from anything such as funerals to divorces. Not so fun. She preferred the forward-looking, wealth management assistance. Here, she could help her customers look for the next house of their dreams, the ideal car, or a grand vacation. Given her decades-long ability to the Beatles.

Her joy didn't come solely from music. She took much pleasure in planting tulip bulbs and early orchids in several of her backyard gardens. She also inevitably would visit her favorite greenhouse in Ardsley, New York.

As a regular, she knew most of the staff and vice-versa. Frank Meyer, the owner of the place, greeted her by her first name. "Margot, nice to see you on this bright Saturday afternoon. Are you looking for something that can spread cheer throughout the inside of the house…and get a head-start on your out-door gardens?"

Maybe both," Margot answered.

juggle numbers, she could often make her clients' dreams come true. Not surprisingly, it was her favorite part of the job.

However, it was not a breeze. It took the ability to truly assess her client's needs….and assess the dollars and cents that were accessible (or borrowable). It required financial acuity. Often, would take several days to respond with a positive answer. Very occasionally, she would need to tell her clients that their request was denied by the higher authorities.

Inevitably, there would be a few surprises in the day. Perhaps a teller would refer a customer who needed immediate financial assistance. Occasionally, she could figure out a way, but occasionally, she would be overruled by the NYC office.

Hopefully, such dashed hopes would not be the last meeting of the day. When it was, she would head home, listen to some spring songs like "It Might As Well Be Spring," by Frank Sinatra and smell the orchids on the table. Instinctively, she would begin smiling again.

# Chapter 2

# *A Fresh Start*

The next day at the bank, Margot had a 9:15 appointment with a fifteen-year Citibank client named Cliff Sanders. Not knowing him well, she asked her secretary to pull out his file and quickly reviewed it before he walked into her office.

"Ms. Roberts....Cliff Sanders," he said when he walked to her desk and introduced himself with a hearty handshake.

"Mr. Sanders, nice to meet you," she said.

"Call me Cliff, " he responded.

"How can I help you?" she asked.

"A fresh start," he responded, as if he had rehearsed the line. " I've been a client of Citibank for perhaps twenty years. Thanks you the bank's help, I have succeeded in running a successful Toyota dealership in Yonkers, New York. Fortunately, Toyota has been a good selling car. But relax, I am not trying to sell you a Toyota Carolla or a Rav 4 today."

"Good, " Margot responded. "I don't need a new car right now."

"That's great," he retorted, "But I could use a new start right about now."

"Such as?" she asked.

"I am thinking about selling my successful dealership, and restarting my mid-life."

"Wow," she innocently said. "Impressive....I guess. What... and why?" "Here's the why: I have the most successful dealership in Westchester County. What more do I want? The most successful dealership in all of New York?

Look at my file, you'll see."

"I did take a quick look at it," Margot answered. "It looks as if you have a gangbuster business."

"Exactly," he agreed.

"And…" she probed.

"I am 55. I still have my health. I have a happy marriage."

"Congratulations," Margot smiled.

"And I still have two kids who live in the area."

'You're lucky," she said. "So why give it up?"

With a smile, Cliff reached in his attaché, and pulled out several sheets of paper. They contained some sketches of sunsets, pastels of NYC bridges, and some portraits of young people (presumably his kids).

"Beautiful," she smiled.

"That's what my high school and college teachers thought…but I decided to postpone that until I had enough money in the bank. I've had several art shows, and they are well-received. I think it's time for me to be an full-time artist," Cliff answered.

"What does your wife think?"

"She loves my paintings, and wants to see me happy as I get older."

Margot took a deep breath, and then looked again at his financial file…partly to stall for time. Yes, if he got a good price for his Toyota dealership, he would have plenty of money to retire for life. And if he sold a few paintings, he might actually enjoy the upcoming decades of his life.

"You're a lucky, talented guy," Margot encouraged him.

"So you think with my equity at Citibank, I can make this transition?" he asked.

"I can almost guarantee it," she answered. "Hopefully, you will get close to your asking price…and if you do, you will have a monthly income about equal to what you now have."

"And if I sell a few pieces of art each month, I may be able to buy my kids an ice cream cone," he chuckled.

"You may be able to buy them more than that" she smiled, and told him that she would most likely have an answer for him tomorrow about a monthly payout of his Citibank savings.

Thanks to her encouragement to the Citibank headquarters, the deal went through.

Margot quietly envied him, and even hoped she might one day buy one of his paintings.

The rest of her day at Citi was consumed with arranging loans for young families looking to buy their first house. She also helped a mother set up an account for her teenage son who would need access to cash during his freshman year in college. On the sad side, she did help a couple gain enough cash from their savings so they could pay for their grandmother's funeral and burial.

It was a typical day for Margot. She felt she had by and large helped customers going through a crossroads in their lives. However, her assistance to Cliff the artist somehow made a special impression on her. The whole idea of regenerating one's life stuck in her brain for the next several hours. Truth be told, it resonated for several days… even months.

# Chapter 3

## *Just Like Starting Over*

THAT EVENING, MARGOT DECIDED TO PARLAY HER inspirational day at Citibank with some action, For starters, she watered all the orchids and lilies in her house. The fresh smell alone made her feel refreshed. She even took a quick walk in her backyard gardens to see a few shoots that were poking their sprouts above the ground.

Looking at the sky, she saw a few patches of blue through the white clouds. It was enough to bring on a smile.

Once inside the house, she decided to continue this rejuvenation with music.

She looked through her stack of LP's and found one title that could match her upward hopes. It was the John Lennon song, "Just Like Starting Over." To be perfectly honest, she wasn't completely familiar with the song, but imagined that it must deal with her headset of rebirth.

Sitting in her easy chair, she began to listen to the tune and the lyrics:

Our life together is so precious together
We have grown. We have grown.
But when I see you darling
It's like we both are falling in love again.
It'll be just like starting over.
Starting over.

Everyday we used to make it love
Why can't we be making love nice and easy
It's time to spread our wings and fly
Don't let another day go by my love
It'll be just like starting over.
Starting over.

It was obviously the wrong sentiment for Margot's mood. Instead of addressing a brand new start, it emotionally conjured the good old days with her late husband George. Margot got up from her easy chair and turned off the record player. She also grabbed a nearby hankie and wiped away her tears.

Not surprisingly, a kaleidoscope of lost memories flooded into her heart. It was not a path to rebirth.

As she reluctantly reminded herself, her dear George was gone. He was not coming back. It was counterproductive to dwell on days that were lost forever.

In the silence of her house, she poured herself a cup of tea and tried to change the subject. Enough music. She turned on the TV, and listened to the latest sad headlines of the day. Damn, there was no escape anywhere. With her remote, she turned off the latest stories of mass killings and political chaos.

Margot then warmed up a pasta dish from the night before and ate alone at the dining room table. She also poured herself another glass of wine and dined in silence.

After about thirty minutes, she decided to open her mail just to escape the loneliness. There were catalogues from Bas Bleu and Hammacher Schlemmer.

There were also bills from Verizon and Con Edison. Not much to take her mind off her down mood. Wait! What was this? An unsolicited mailing from Silver Singles.

She vaguely knew of this dating site for people over the age of 50. When she opened the envelope and read the pitch, she discovered that more than 50,000 senior citizens signed up every week. The bottom line on the letter summed up her mood: As it said, "Why not give it a try? What do you have to lose?"

Since Dear George had passed away, she had met up with some neighborhood widowers once or twice at holiday parties but had never really been on a "date."

She poured herself another tea and silently wondered if this was perhaps a path to rebirth. For some strange reason, she proceeded to fill out the questionnaire…answering her weight, body type, religion, and ideal escapes. In some ways, it was a personality test—one she ironically enjoyed.

True, she did her best to assess the personalities of her clients so as to better serve their needs. However, no one really seemed to quiz her about her personality,

# CHAPTER 4

## *Annie calls.*

A CALL FROM 25-YEAR OLD ANNIE ROBERTS ALWAYS lifted Margot's spirits.

Mom was immensely proud of her daughter's Master's Degree from prestigious British universities.

Since her graduation, she had started a well-paying job at Unilever in London, where the company has its head office. During her master's program, she had studied marketing, which came in handy at this corporation. Her exact job?

Assistant Marketing director of Dove and Vaseline Petroleum Jelly.

Every time she called to speak with her mom, it was a thrill for both of them. However, this particular call had a slightly different tone.

"I know, but I have possible new path," the daughter said. "I got a call out of nowhere last week from Google, who may be interested in hiring me. A friend of mine from college works there, and seems to be always beaming when I am with her. She suggested it might be a launch pad for a brave new world."

"Well, as I tell all my clients at Citibank, I don't think one should ever say no to a new overture for a possible job." "I agree…so I met with the chief marketing director last week," Annie answered.

"And how did it go?"

"He seemed to like my enthusiasm, and may get back to me this week."

"Geez…"Margot reacted.

"Who knows how it will go. But it's worth a try. It might be fun to find out if there is a more exciting path out there for me," the daughter explained.

"Yikes,…you're only 28."

"No, no, no….I am just trying to better understand this curious journey of happiness."

"It's a long journey," Margot interjected.

"I just think I need to experience a new, fresh start." Annie answered."

However, she looked at the bottom line of the mailer and quietly nodded: "What do you have to lose?"

"You would not be disappointed if I chased it."

"No, no, no. Win or lose, I am proud of you." Mom said lovingly.

After a pause, Annie responded. "I had a hunch that would be what your might say. I know you, mom. You seem to always support reinventing yourself, and "I know, mom, but I don't want to wait until I am 53 to figure out what's next." "Are you talking about your dear mother?" Margot instinctively answered.

experiencing new things. Otherwise, you would have never supported me going to school in London."

"Well, you are too kind, Annie." The mother answered. "Check it out, honey. If it doesn't feel right. walk away from it. But give it a shot. As I read the other day in a pitch to me, 'What do you have to lose?'"

"Mom, you are the best." Annie gushed.

"Keep me posted," Margot replied.

"I love you," Annie answered.

"I love you back." the mother heard a kiss over the phone line and then a hang-up. As she hung up the phone, she couldn't help but think that today's generation was attracted to opportunities somewhere over the rainbow. She wondered if she shouldn't be more attentive to those types of new opportunities in her own life.

# CHAPTER 5

## *Kindred spirit?*

A FEW DAYS LATER, SHE GOT AN EARLY response from a gentleman on Silver Singles. His name was Mike Baldwin and it seemed innocent enough, although she did wonder if she was out of her mind even participating on this site.

Mike explained that he was 54, had been divorced for ten years, and had no children. Good enough, she told herself. He lived in Tarrytown, New York, which was only about ten minutes from her home in Dobbs Ferry. So far, so good. Then he wrote that he too was a banking executive… at Chase in White Plains. As he explained, he was the managing director, so according to him "we won't have to waste a lot of time explaining what we do for a living." Yikes!

It's not like she didn't care to hear his take on the job, but perhaps it was too identical to her own career path. Oh well, it beat other overtures…including a man in New Jersey was currently separated from his wife of 23 years. That was a situation that Margot did not want to intrude upon. There was another response here often?"

"Well, yeah. It's close to me. They have good appetizers, and excellent drinks. Would you like a dinner here? " "Oh, I think just a little bite and maybe a drink." She retorted.

By then, the waitress came to the table and also greeted Mike by his first name. "Would you like the usual, Mike," she asked.

"Oh, I think maybe some cheese and crackers for the table. I'll have a Vodka from a man in Peekskill, New York who was an Uber driver. He was 67 years old. Too much of a gap, Margot thought.

Margot had to admit that Mike the banker was probably the easiest connection, although she was still cautious. She reminded herself of the Silver Singles motto: What do you have to lose?

In preparation for her Saturday night date, she went to her favorite greenhouse and consulted with Frank, the owner.

"Margot, Margot…so nice to see you again," he said. "What can I do for you?"

"I might like some potted spring flowers that smell nice," she answered with a smile.

"That's a great idea. Follow me."

Margot walked along with Frank and felt brighter and more beautiful just seeing and smelling the plants. "Are you going to keep them in the house for a few weeks until you plant them outside.

"That's the idea. You can read my mind," she answered.

"Try these. The primrose are beautiful and will flourish all summer long. And so will these daffodils. Give them sunlight."

I think they are gorgeous and will certainly brighten my living room until I plant them in my front garden," she reacted. "I'll take both of them, Frank."

As Frank was walking to his register, he started whistling "Here Comes the Sun."

"Well, Frank….you're a cheerful soul this Saturday morning."

"Actually, Margot, I am usually pretty cheerful. I've been doing this for decades, and it normally doesn't depress me. Maybe only when I have to pay the bills."

"I know that feeling, especially from my clients at the bank. But I am glad you feel good about the day to day. As she reached in her billfold to pay the cashier, she thanked him for the flowers, and walked them to the car. Along the way, she started to whistle the happy tune that Frank had started.

Once she got home, she put both those potted plants on each side of the fireplace, and played some upbeat music on her record player. It was a good morning.

When Mike arrived at 7:30 p.m. for their Silver Singles get-to-gether, she opened the door with a cheerful expression. He extended his hand for a handshake and introduced himself.

"Wow, it's a beautiful home," he smiled.

"Well, I try," Margot shrugged. "Would you like a cocktail before we head out?"

"No, I don't think so. I called Red Hat restaurant to see if they were crowded yet, and they weren't…but if we go much later, it gets packed, and then it's a little hard to chat. So, I think it might be best if we get on our way."

The drive to Red Hat in Irvington was an easy one in Mike's Lincoln. He mentioned that he had had a busy week, and was looking forward to an escape with her.

"How was your week," he asked.

"Good. About the same as usual," she answered.

It was small talk mostly. Of course, that shouldn't surprise her. After all, it had been decades since she had been on a real date. When they arrived at the restaurant, Mike escorted her into the place. Once inside, he greeted the person at the front desk, who knew him by his first name. "Your usual table?" she asked.

"That would be great," Mike answered.

Once they were seated, Margot asked the inevitable question. "You come here often?"

"It's close to me and food is great, " Mike nodded. As he did so, the waitress came to the table. "Mike, what will it be tonight. Can I bring you both a drink while you look at the menu. Mike responded, "I'll have a vodkaon the rocks. And you Margot?"

"I'll have a glass of Rose wine," she answered and looked around the restaurant. It was a pretty place right on the Hudson River, and was quickly filling up with people, as Mike had predicted.

The next half-hour was not easy. Mike seemed to turn every attempt at easy conversation into a banking discussion. For example, "Have you ever been to Paris?" Answer: "Yes, the Eiffel Tower is pretty…and we have a beautiful Chase office near there." Another example: "Isn't Rio pretty?" Answer: The beaches are beautiful, and we have a great Chase office only one block from the ocean."

Finally, Margot decided to probe. Sipping her wine, she asked him "Not to get too personal, but why did your marriage end up in divorce?" He took another sip of his second vodka and sighed. "My wife Rosie wanted to go the all the Broadway plays and musicals. She even liked matinees. As you probably know, you can't do that if you are dedicated to your job as a banker."

Ay, yi, yi! This was worse than she ever imagined. Every once in a while, she looked at her watch, and finally told Mike, "I should get home. I promised to call my sister tonight."

It wasn't true. She didn't even have a sister, but she didn't want this ordeal to continue.

Immediately, Mike motioned to the waitress, who approached the table. "Hi, Helen," he said. "Just put this on my bill."

He then walked Margot to his Lincoln and like a gentleman, opened the passenger door. All the way home, they chatted about banking, and when they reached her front door, Mike did give her a kiss on the cheek.

Margot forced a smile, thanked him for the evening, and headed into her Banking executive, which is what he liked to call himself. It was also the last time for at least a month that she would respond to an entreaty from Silver Single beautifully scented living room. It was the last time she would speak with the Chase

# CHAPTER 6

## *Back to work.*

THE NEXT WEEK WAS BUSINESS AS USUAL at Citibank. That's not to suggest that it was completely depressing week. Margot helped arrange a loan for a struggling thirty-something couple who needed to expand their bungalow to accommodate their only living grandparent. She also helped transfer funds for an affluent customer to her son, who had served in the US Army, and now wanted to relocate in Florida.

Her hi-light of the week was a surprise Friday visit from Cliff, Sanders who had an excellent offer for his Toyota dealership. She was glad to see him. "Have a seat," she said. "Tell me all about it."

"Actually, it's my second offer of the week, and much better than the first."

He had written the dollar figure on a piece of paper and shoved it across the desk to Margot. It was well over two-million dollars.

Margot had done her homework on her client's behalf. Over the past few weeks, she had researched auto dealership prices, and discovered that anything over 1.5 million was a considered a generous, acceptable offer.

"So far, that sounds pretty good," she responded with a smile.

"That's exactly what my wife says," he answered. "What will I need to do next?"

"Well, you need to go to lawyer, unless you already have. I will need to give you a balance sheet for your business."

"You already have," he reminded her.

"And you will need a balance sheet from the person who wants to buy you out."

"Such as?"

"Assets. Fiinancial debt. Investments at banks or brokerage firms. Terms you would like. For example, would you like the person to pay you in one lump sum…or over 5-10 years."

"I might like half the money up front. Then I could spread the remainder out over the next five years."

"It might take a few months," Margot cautioned him.

"I realize that."

"Do you have enough art ideas to move forward?"

He laughed. "I have enough art ideas for decades."

Margot couldn't help but react. "Cliff, I am so proud of you."

"Thanks. So am I. So is my wife. We think we will never be happier."

"I hope so. By the way, do you have an art website?"

Cliff reached in his pocket and pulled out a business card. "Here it is. Cliff Sanders, artist." After a pause, he smiled. "I like the sound of that."

"Keep in touch," Margot said.

"You know I will," Cliff said and exited her office with a thumbs-up. She repeated the gesture and was sincerely happy for him and his wife.

Later that evening, Margot walked in her house feeling she had done a good thing for a client she admired. She then watered the plants and took in sweet smell of all her new daffodils and primroses.

She then put on some rejuvenating songs including "Brand New Day," and "We've Only Just Begun."

Then she decided to cook a good meal from scratch. After looking at several of her favorite cookbooks, she made a meatloaf and butternut squash. It was surprisingly delicious and she vowed to make more meals from scratch.

Before she tucked in, she took a walk in her backyard, and considered what she might do to keep this mood alive. Ah, the air smelled good. After considering many options, she decided to explore two new paths that could fill her Saturday and Sunday. She hoped both of these venues would be open for her over the weekend, and decided to check on them first thing in the morning.

For the first time in many days, she went to sleep with a smile on her face.

# CHAPTER 7

## *Bon Appetit.*

On Saturday, Margot called Sur La Table to see if they had any available spots for a cooking class. She was a decent cook, but did not often prepare fancy dishes, especially since she was now alone in her home. However, she did enjoy the process and the social aspect of such a class. She had taken a few classes decades ago with her late husband and enjoyed the experience. As a single person now, she wondered if it would be as enriching, but somehow believed the smells of fresh baking, and the creativity of new recipes could be refreshing.

The person on the phone told her that they did have some open spots for an afternoon class that started at 2 p.m. " It's a three and half hour class where you are teamed in a group of four or five people, and together you create a full meal."

"Do I need to bring an apron?" Margot asked.

"No, we supply everything—including the ingredients and utensils. And you don't even have to clean the dishes afterwards!"

Margot laughed at the bonus. "Wow, this sounds more attractive the more you explain it."

"Have you ever taken a cooking class?"

"About a decade ago," Margot answered.

"Well, the recipes are pretty international now, and most people love it. I'll bet you will too. "

Margot agreed to attend, and looked forward to an experience outside the home that might rejuvenate her spirits.

About five minutes before 2, she arrived at the Sur La Table address which was in the Ridge Hill shopping center only about five minutes from her home. There were about six or seven people already waiting in the lobby. In the next five minutes, three more people joined and were escorted to the kitchen.

Not surprisingly, it was pristine and totally modern. At the top of the kitchen classroom, there was a chef who introduced herself as Shelly. She also introduced two young chef helpers named Bobby and Carol. And then she introduced the staff that would be cleaning up the mess after the class had prepared the meals.

"OK, you know who we are," Shelly then said. "You're going to be working as a team, but please introduce yourself and if possibly explain what you hope to get out of this class."

Margot looked at her fellow students and guessed that most of them were about 30 years old. A few of them were more middle-aged, like Margot, and there were even a few that appeared to be in the seventies.

Why were they there?

The answers were as varied as the individual classmates.

"I wanted to become a better cook for parties."

" Just to escape the daily grind."

and an older gentleman named Carl.

Shelly, the head chef then explained that each group should divide their tasks, and be assisted with a chef assistant (their group's assistant chef was Bobby. Shelly then handed out a ten-page recipe collection that explained what would be

"Just for fun."

"I have travelled some parts of the world, and like the international flavor of this class."

When it was Margot's turn, she explained her intentions. "At this stage of my life, I would like to feel rejuvenated…and think cooking may be a way."

Each of the other students gave their hopes for the class, and then Shelly divided the class into two groups of five. In Margot's group, there were two young folks named Charlie and Betty. There was another middle-aged woman named June and an older gentleman named. Carl.

The dishes were as follows: Watermelon Gazpacho. Pao de Quejo de Rio for starters, Beef Wellington as the main course, and Tarte Tatin for dessert. In the confines of her group, Margot volunteered to handle the dessert, since she had always loved to bake.

The older gentleman hoped to prepare the gazpacho, since the recipe looked relatively easy. June, the other middle-aged woman volunteered to make the Pao de Quijo. A puffy cheese bread. That left the two younger students.

Bobby, the chef's assistant, suggested that they work together on the Beef Wellington, since it required more ingredients and was a little more involved. Bobby then clapped his hands together and encouraged the students in his group, "Let's get going. Let's make some tasty masterpieces."

Margot instinctively felt is was a nicely varied group, and an enticing menu.

She began by peeling the apples, coring them and cutting them in half. Then she rolled the puff pastry into a sheet that would fit easily inside a pie plate. In fact, there was enough for two pie plates. As instructed in the recipe, she poked holes into the pastry.

To the apples, she added some teaspoons of water, a cup of sugar, and 6 teaspoons of butter. In a saucepan, she cooked them until they were amber in color....about 15-20 minutes. When the liquid was caramelized, she took the saucepan off the heat.

Now the tricky part: she then poured the apples into two pie tins and covered them with the puffed pastry, pushing the edges down all around the gooey apple mixture.

At last, it was oven time! She baked both dishes for about 45-50 minutes. When she took them out, the smell wafted through the entire kitchen. As directed, she let it cool for about and hour. During this time, she helped the partners in her group with cutting ingredients or monitoring the ovens.

As Shelly had earlier warned each group, she would give them a five-minute.

According to both groups who tasted everything, Margot's apple tarte was the hit of the cooking class. It was considered by most as prettier and more fragrant than the ones baked across the kitchen by another students.

Over the classroom feast, there was a lot of easy chitchat between all the people who participated. When it was time to go, Chef Shelly congratulated all the warning to plate each of their dishes and prepare for a group meal. At the end of five minutes, she announced, "Let's eat!"

By god, the entire meal was great. She particularly enjoyed the watermelon gazpacho, and complimented Carl, the most senior person in the group, The other dishes were also delicious…but the hit of the entire meal seemed to be the Tarte Tatin, that Margot had prepared.

The participants, and as usual, divided all the remaining food so each person could have an additional taste later at night.

By 5:30, they all gave each other a hug and headed home. Later that night, Margot had a small bite of each dish and congratulated herself in silence. Yes, it was all good….but not so thrilling to enjoy it in a lonely dining room. Somehow, it was enough to recall her last class, when she cooked as a couple with George. Oh well, no point living in the past. No, this would not be the solution to her private, enduring wanderlust.

# CHAPTER 8

## *The Botanical Gardens.*

IT HAD BEEN A WHILE SINCE MARGOT had been to the New York Botanical Gardens. After her husband had died, she had started going to the local Greenhouse to replenish her many outdoor gardens and bring some sweet aromas into her home. However, she had never been to the Botanical Garden with George, so in a weird way, it was always new.

Sunday happened to be a beautiful spring day for her exploratory. Once she was past the entry gate, the green grass and the barely blooming trees signaled the start of a new season.

When she reached the conservatory, she decided to enter and walk the rows of cascading plants and small trees around every corner. Given the beauty and scents, it was hard not to feel more alive and aware of the world. There were dozens of magnolias leading to a few flowering dogwoods. Down the way, she could see magnolias and azaleas just below yellow forsythias. In fact, every direction she looked, she could see colors and smell scents.

Once she walked out the back door of the conservatory, she discovered the small lakes with gentle fountains. Absolutely beautiful!

Outside this display, she jumped on the tram and visited some as yet unseen attractions, including the annual orchid show, which showcased an array of pink and purple hues.

Inspired by her visit, she went to the office to see if the place had classes that might interest her. Lo and behold, they had many.

An easy subject matter was landscape design. Here, she could study and learn how plants could be partnered. Another possibility was grading and drainage.

There was another subject matter that seemed even more up her alley. It was called therapeutic horticulture classes. The class promised to help students to create experiences that utilize plants, gardening and nature to empower individuals and groups. As the blurb says, "whether you are embarking on a new career or looking to integrate plants into your current work in human services, education, mental health or other allied health fields, our expert faculty—all highly experienced practitioners–are the ideal guides." The class also promised to be useful for people with illnesses, injuries, disabilities or other maladies.

While Margot didn't have any of these particular problems, she did like the theme of these classes. The catalogue even suggested set it could help students set up, operate and effectively market a business that offers therapeutic services.

Obviously, she was a long way from that…but the glorious objective seemed attractive to her.

Before she left the Botanical Gardens, she asked for calendar for all their upcoming classes. They even had classes in botanical art and illustration, floral design, gardening, and urban naturalism—all of which sounded interesting to her.

Before she left the New York Botanical Gardens, she even visited the children's garden, where she saw you kids giggling with their parents and feeling closer to nature.

It was a good afternoon. She bought a few books on gardening from the NYBG bookstore, and she promised herself to take a class or two, and perhaps even ask Frank at the Greenhouse if he had any specific suggestions.

That evening, she watered all the plants in the house and found a movie on HBO called "Greenfingers." It was a complete garden-oriented day.

Amazingly, it did not feel like overkill. At a decent hour, she went to sleep and felt inspired to actually help people tomorrow at the bank.

# CHAPTER 9

## *Another day, another dollar.*

THE NEXT WEEK WAS ANOTHER TYPICAL STRETCH at Citibank. As usual, she got lots of calls from customers asking her to transfer money from savings to checking. There were a few requests to move some money from Citibank to brokerage firms, and vice versa. She was a pro at doing all these transactions, since she had done.

At school, my son and another son got in a fist fight. Cops came and one of them them for years. It was a lot of paperwork, but completely necessary.

She vastly preferred meeting face-to-face with customers and trying to solve their needs. Most of these were life-style transitions, and Margot had learned early on that she was a good listener for such topics. She could assess the needs they might have, and often suggest a few financial routes that might make their dreams possible.

Example? A thirty-something man named Paul had an appointment with Margot early in the week. He had been a customer at Citibank for about a decade, and operated 3 food carts in Elmsford, Bronxville, and outside the train station in Yonkers.

Paul explained that it was a work-intensive business, but it did return a decent living. His busiest hours were early in the morning, noontime, and the after work hours. On each of his food carts, he had a few workers who could help make scrambled eggs, flip hamburgers, and make some pasta—sometimes for customers who wanted "to go" food.

Margot looked over his spreadsheets for the businesses. "Each of them look pretty good, "she complimented him. "What's on your mind? Do you want to start a new food cart and need a quick loan?"

"No, it's more ambitious than that," he answered. "I'd actually like to start a restaurant where I could create and serve more ambitious dishes."

"And do you want to sell the food carts?"

"Not necessarily. As you can see, they all return a profit…and I have some good employees who could operate them. I found a good smallish store-front in White Plains, where I could operate a more adventurous sit-down restaurant."

"How much is it." she asked

"The rent is five-thousand a month…but I would need to redecorate it and hire a new staff." After a pause, he added. "As you can see, I have some savings here…but I may need a loan to make a go of it."

Margot looked back at his files and saw that he had never missed a home loan payment and had grown his savings year after year. "It may be possible," she said and asked him to get a firm figure on his locations and better estimates on the improvements he would need to make. "I will try to make it happen for you," she then responded with a smile.

With a slight hooray gesture, he shook Margot's hand, said "Thank you," and exited the bank with some pep in his step.

Another client mid-week had an appointment for a rather significant loan. Her name was Esther Blake. A fortyish African-American woman and she appeared right on time.

She pulled up a chair in Margot's office and explained her sad situation. "My son Terry is in jail, and I would like to get him a good lawyer so he can be free…but lawyers are expensive."

"Oh yes, they can be." Margot agreed from first hand experience with her late husband.

"What's your son being held in jail for?"

"Dousing a cop with fire extinguisher spray.

"Yikes, that's not so good,"

"I know," Esther said, but added, "It's a little more complicated than that. My son got in a fight with a fellow classmate. Cops came. One took out his tazer and tazed my son in the leg. My son found a fire extinguisher on the wall and unleashed it on the cop. Another cop handcuffed him and arrested him, "Oh, boy." Margot reacted. "At least, he didn't shoot the cop with a gun."

"He doesn't have a gun, thank god. But he's in jail until the trial."

Have you tried to get legal aid?" She looked at Esther's balance sheet and saw that she was very middle-class person.

"Yes," Esther answered and brought out a hanky to wipe away her tears. "Evidently, I make a little too much to qualify for that."

Margot looked at her balance sheet and had to agree. She didn't have a lot of money, but she was above any poverty line. "Let me think," she said and held up her hand to get her thoughts together. Her advice was that it would certainly cost money, but perhaps she could stretch out the legal payments over many years.

She then took out a sheet of paper and scribbled a name and number. It was her late husband's boss at the law firm, and the phone number.

"Call this man tomorrow and explain that you are a friend of mine. Tell him you are short of cash, but will be good for the fee if he could stretch payments to him over 2-3 years. It's worth a try."

"I'll definitely give it a try." Esther said and left the office in tears.

Later that afternoon, Margot called her husband's old law firm and asked the man if he could take on an important client and extend repayments over several years. The banker said she would try to back the loan. The lawyer promised he would do his best, and explained a few pleasantries with Margot.

Her last face-to-face appointment of the week was with a 60-year old couple who wanted some advice relocating from Peekskill to Ft. Lauderdale, Florida.

"A retirement home," Margot asked.

"I don't know," the wife answered. "We both may work down there. After all these years, we just want a change of scene.

"As I understand it,, Ft. Lauderdale real estate may be cheaper than Westchester," Margot offered.

"That's what we hear. We're going to explore down there over the next month, and will keep you posted. I just wanted to alert you in advance."

"Well, if you find something you like, I will try to expedite things for you, and wish you all the best."

As you can tell, it wasn't all grunt work. On many days, Margot felt she was helping people in the important junctions of their lives. However, the bulk of her days were pushing paper and adding columns of numbers. More important, several decades of this had begun to feel like "the same old thing."

Perhaps someday, things could change. Perhaps someday, she could feel as good as she made others feel.

# CHAPTER **10**

## *Annie has news.*

"Mom?" the young woman on the other side of the telephone asked. "Annie?" "Yep, your one and only." The daughter answered.

"What's new?"

"Some good stuff."

"Such as…" Margot pleaded.

"I took that new job," Annie answered with a happy tone.

After a pause, her mom pressed for more. "Wow, Tell me all about it."

Her daughter took a breath and then answered. "Well, you know it's with Google. But let me walk you through the last few weeks. Somehow, Unilever got wind of the fact that I was not so happy there. So my boss there called me into his office and suggested they could maybe add another product to my portfolio."

"Exciting," Margot answered sarcastically.

"Their suggestion? Lifebuoy soap."

"Your dad used to love that brand."

"It's intended for people in that age group, " Annie answered. "But wait…there's more. They also said I could maybe get a raise in the next twenty-four months."

"Wow, they really appreciate you."

"Past tense, mom."

"Go on."

"Over the last week, I had three interviews at Google.

"Promising," Margot encouraged.

"The first one was a woman who was the head of human resources. She liked me…and wanted me to interview a few nights later with the head of advertising and promotion. I agreed to do so."

"And…."

"And I was a hit. He said they had interviewed twenty people, and I was his favorite."

"So…"

"So he told me that I would soon hear from him. Two days later he called, and offered me the job at 25% more money than I was making at Unilever."

"Wow. You must be good."

"I guess I take after my mother. The best thing mom, is that this new gig feels like an exciting fresh start. I had already exhausted everything that I could try at Unilever. I know they could throw new products and assignments my way…but they are all pretty much the same. This new job at Google promises to be a fresh start into the future."

"I am so proud of you," the mother instantly responded.

After a pause, Annie spoke again. "I have one other thing to speak with you about."

"Don't tell me you are getting married."

"No, not yet. But I do have a boyfriend or two."

"Good. What's the news?

"I have some days off before I need to start my new job, and I wonder if you could come and visit me in London,, Annie said. "I have plenty of room for you to stay, and I don't need to start until May 12."

"Maybe you might prefer to come to New York and see me," Margot suggested.

"I really can't. I need to tie up some loose ends still at Unilever for a few days, and I will need to complete some paperwork for my new job at Google. But I will be free for the Friday and the entire weekend. Besides, mom, last I spoke with you, you sounded like maybe you could use a change of scene. Please say yes….I'd love to see you."

Margot looked at her calendar, and felt it would be relatively easy to take off those days. After all, she had enough seniority at Citibank, and would truly love to see her daughter.

"That's a deal," she replied. "I will try to come in on Thursday night, and spend the entire weekend with you, my dear."

"That's the greatest, mom. I can't wait to see you," Annie enthusiastically answered.

"Perfect! I'll call you back with my flight details. Meanwhile, enjoy the transition."

"Oh, I really am, " her daughter said. And mom, I really look forward to seeing you, but I have to get off the line now."

"Fine, I love you babe." The mother said.

"Love you back," Annie said and hung up.

After the call, Margot smiled and booked her trip with Expedia. She looked forward to spending some time with dear daughter. She did have one little concern: The statement from Anna that perhaps mom needed a change of scene. My god, was the sameness of her routine that obvious? Perhaps it was. If so, the trip to London might be the tonic she needed…at least, temporarily.

# CHAPTER 11

## *London with fresh eyes.*

I N THE MIDDLE OF THE NEXT WEEK, Margot called Annie to share her weekend flight plans and discuss a rough idea of things to do in London.

"I was thinking we might see a play or musical Friday night," Annie offered.

"You know I like musicals," mom responded.

"I looked in the newspaper and have some ideas, Annie Suggested. "How about Phantom of the Opera, Les Miserables, Moulin Rouge, the King and I, Oklahoma. Any of those make your boat float?"

After a pause, Margot responded as gently as possible. "Actually, no," she retorted. "They all seem like productions of another long ago era. I'd prefer something newer and fresher. "I saw online that there is a new musical playing called "Lemons, Lemons, Lemons, Lemons, Lemons." It might be exciting to see something a little out of the ordinary. What do you say?"

"I've honestly never heard of it, but I'm game if you are," the daughter answered. "I'll look it up and try to get some tickets for Friday night,"

"Great," mom responded. "We'll figure out other stuff to do when we get together.

"Sounds great."

"Can't wait."

After their phone conversation, Margot explored what other things they might enjoy doing together in London. Fact is, she had been to London at least six of seven times—many times with her late husband, and several times with Annie as she was preparing for college.

Margot had seen most of the tried-and-true sights. She didn't really want to spend her time in the Natural History Museum, Buckingham Palace, the Tower of London, Westminster Abbey, or any of the other century old attractions. She thought it might be fun to spend some time at Borough Market, Covent Gardens, and the London Eye. Instead of the British Museum, she hoped they could visit the Tate Modern and see some newer pieces of art. Given her interest in gardening, she did think a trip to Key Gardens could be refreshing. There were a few other things on her list, but she hoped to discuss them with Annie.

When she arrived at her daughter's nice apartment late Thursday night in the Soho section of London, they gave each other a hug and looked forward to a few days together. Annie poured her mom a glass of wine and wondered how the trip was.

"Great, great , great," Mom responded. "I did my best to not fall asleep on the flight so I would not get too off-kilter with the time zone difference."

"That's great mom. You look great. What's new? How's the banking world?"

Margot sighed. "Oh, you know, honey. It's basically the same old thing. I've been doing it now for almost 30 years. The financial advice I give people is basically the same as I gave them in 1990's… it just involves more money these days. I envy you, my dear Annie, since you have the courage to reinvent your life without spending 30 years selling the same old laundry detergent for Unilever."

"Well, hopefully this weekend will give you a breath of fresh air," Annie said and toasted her mom. "I got tickets to that weird, new musical you wanted to see. It's for tomorrow night."

"Perfect."

"I thought we might get in one of those black taxicabs and visit a bunch of sights tomorrow. Have you seen the British Museum, mom?"

"Many times."

"How about the Tower of London?"

"Been there. Done that."

"How about the London Roman Wall? Evidently, it was built about 200 AD."

"Wow, that's a long time ago. No, I'd prefer to do some newer things," Margot answered. "For starters, I'd rather not sit in a black cab for hours or a double-decker bus." I saw on the web that London now has electric bicycles for rent. Have you ever been on one?"

"Nope." Annie answered. "I do have a regular bicycle, but only one. And those electric bikes do look fun."

"They look fun to me, too," mom agreed. "And it could give us a chance to see the city in a brand new way. "

"Honey, have you ever been on the London Eye?" mom suggested.

"That big ferris wheel? I've passed it by many times, but never been on it." Annie admitted.

"Let's do it together. "

I might also like to go to the Tate Modern museum. Evidently, they have a brand new exhibit featuring Jenny Holzer's avant garde artwork."

"Wow, mom, you have turned into Ms. Modern! " Annie exclaimed.

"I'm trying babe, Don't want to live in the past."

"Well, I have one thing I would definitely like to do Sunday afternoon before your return flight."

"Tell me."

"I'd like to introduce you to one of my boyfriends. His name is Adam—a lawyer like dad. But we thought it would be fun to go to Kew Gardens and see their new exhibits, and then have lunch there. Is that too old-fashioned for you?"

Mom smiled. "Honey, I would love to do that. I have taken a new interest in gardening…and I would definitely like to meet this guy Adam. Serious relationship?"

"We've gone out for about seven months, but I have a few other male friends as well," she admitted. "Even so, Adam is fun, and I thought you might enjoy each other."

"That's a deal," Margot remarked.

"Tomorrow, let's make it an easy day," her daughter suggested. We'll wake up whenever you wake up. No alarms clocks. Maybe we'll grab a quick lunch in the neighborhood. Then the play, 'Lemons, lemons, lemons, lemons, lemons.' I say we take a taxi there…and save the electric bikes for Saturday. Zoom. Zoom. Zoom," Agree?"

The next day, as Annie could have predicted, her mom did get up late, but well rested without much jet-lag. They took a nice stroll in the neighborhood and visited a few shops. After trying on a few new clothes and resisting the temptation to buy some trinkets, they did stop into on of Annie's favorite local restaurants and enjoyed some fish and chips. During the meal, Margot quizzed her daughter about her ambitions and hopes for her new job at Google.

"I mostly like the fact that it is my window to a brave new world, " Annie answered. "I know a little about the tech business, but not a whole lot…so I imagine I will have a long learning curve, but that's good too."

As Margot listened, she kept nodding and truly admired her daughter's courage and ambition.

Later that day, they did prepare for a night at Harold Pinter Theatre. The show, "Lemons, lemons, etc" was an unconventional, tender and funny rom-com about what we say, how we say it, and what happens when we can't say anything more.

It brought out more than a few laughs from Margot and Annie.

The next day, Annie got up early and rented two electric bikes only a few blocks away. After a few trial runs, mom and daughter, got on their way and did a little sight-seeing in London. Along the way, they did stop at the London Eye and took the 30-minute ferris wheel ride above the Thames. Both had to admit it was quite thrilling.

In the afternoon, they zoomed to the Tate Modern Museum, where they saw new artwork from Jenny Holzer, Much of it was impressionistic and quite striking. Some of it contained words, which Margot found quite innovative and interactive.

An electric bike ride on the paved way along the Thames near sunset was exciting for both. Rather than press their luck zooming in the dark, they did return their electric bikes to the rental site. Over dinner, Annie did acknowledge that it was an exciting fun day…

one she would rarely experience on her own, without her mom's encouragement.

On Sunday, Annie's friend, Adam, came to her apartment to pick up the two-some in his small car. After a cup of tea for all, they headed to Kew Garden to take in a sunny day.

At this time of year, Kew Gardens was stunning. Spring flowers were everywhere and the trees had begun to blossom. In the conservatory, it was even more beautiful. There was no wind inside the building to blow the beautiful blooms.

After an hour or two walk, Margot, Annie and Adam sat down for a lunch on the premises.

Do you come often to Kew Gardens," Margot asked the young man.

"I would say at least once a month," Adam answered.

"Wow, I am impressed," Margot reacted.

"Well, I guess Annie told you that I am a lawyer. Most days, it's researching cases in leather-bound law books. Every once in a while, I look to get a breath of fresh air, and I find that the gardens revitalize me."

"Wow, I feel exactly the same way," Margot answered. "My day to day is not law books, but financial statements. Consequently, I go to the local greenhouse, or the New York Botanical Gardens quite often. I love it."

"You go that often"" Annie asked his mother.

"Sure, it makes me feel renewed."

The threesome enjoyed the lunch, and Adam offered to bring them all home to Annie's residence. While the two younger folks chatted, Margot packed her bags for the trip back to the U.S."

When she came out with her luggage, Adam remarked," I hear the two of you rented electric bikes one day....and enjoyed exploring new things.

"You sure," Annie asked.

"Absolutely." The mom answered.

When the taxi came, Margot gave her daughter a kiss, and feeling happy to meet Adam, she gave him a peck on the lips too. That sounds heavenly.

"Fantastic."

"It was fun," Annie agreed. Looking at her luggage, Adam offered to drive Margot to the airport. "No, no, no,…that's not necessary," the mom said. "Annie, just call me a taxi, and the two of you can have an evening together."

"You sure," Annie asked.

"Absolutely." The mom answered.

When the taxi came, Margot gave her daughter a kiss, and feeling happy to meet Adam, she gave him a peck on the cheek, too.

"It was nice to meet you," Adam said. "Give Annie a little advance warning and we'll go to Kew Gardens again."

As Margot walked out the front door, she blew them all another kiss, and soon headed to Heathrow for the long trip back to Manhattan.

# CHAPTER 12

## *You don't live forever.*

Back in New York, Margot felt buoyed by her trip to London. At least for the first three days of the week, she did not seem bothered by the sameness of work. In fact, she watered all the plants and enjoyed the aroma. She walked around the block every night before sunset. She even baked some cookies and shared them with her next door neighbor, Carol.

To be honest, Margot was not a very neighborly woman. During her marriage and her daughter's high school years, she was preoccupied with her own family. When all that changed, she decided it was too late to initiate new relationships with people who had their own family. True, she would occasionally share cookies with her next-door neighbor, Carol. But to be perfectly honest, it was usually because the recipe called for too many pieces than a woman alone could consume.

When she rang Carol's bell on Wednesday night, she was surprised to see Carol in a rather somber mood. The woman invited her in and appreciated the cookies, but also broke some heartbreaking news.

"Did you hear about Vivian?" Carol asked.

"No," Margot responded. "I've been gone for a few days in London to see my daughter. What's with Vivian?" Margot vaguely knew Vivian, who lived two doors down, next to Carol. She knew that Vivian was a woman in her mid-forties, who had been diagnosed with cancer.

"She died over the weekend," Carol sadly answered.

"No, she was so young."

"Forty-six," Carol said. "Finally, the cancer got her."

"Omigod," Margot responded. "I remember her kids when they still lived at home. Owen used to sometimes shovel the snow out of our driveway. And Brittany was a sweetie."

"Thank god they are all on their own, but they were around the house when their mom passed…and as you may know her husband Gerry moved on and remarried so poor Vivian was basically all on her own," Carol explained.

"I know the feeling," Margot agreed. "What did she do for a living?"

"She worked for the city of Hastings on their administrative staff for the past 24 years. I know she was tired of it, but it was a decent civil service job...and she didn't quite know what else to do."

Margot just nodded in an understanding way.

After a pause, Carol broke the silence. "She is being waked tonight at Edwards-Dowdle. If you would like I'll give you a lift."

"That would be nice," Margot answered., and again repeated that the cookies were just a good neighborly gift. "Enjoy," she said and exited the neighbor's house.

At around 7 p.m., Carol honked her horn in her nextdoor neighbor's driveway, and Margot joined her in the car. Within fifteen minutes, they pulled into the funeral home, and signed the guest book.

It was not a huge crowd. Perhaps 40 people from the neighborhood, and another 30 friends of the kids. Margot looked around the room and recognized only a few people. She did go up to the casket and say a prayer for her departed neighbor, Vivian.

After paying her respects, she was approached by the kids, who recognized her in the crowd. Brittany quickly gave her a hug and thanked her for coming. Owen's acknowledgement was a little longer. He recalled shoveling Margot's snow and appreciated her generous tips.

They shared a little chitchat about the neighborhood, and Owen admitted that he sometimes missed it, since he now lived in Connecticut.

As they were wrapping up the conversation, Margot told him how very sorry she was that he lost his mother, especially since she was so young.

"I appreciate that," Owen nodded. "But mom was sick for while with cancer.

And besides, no one lives forever."

At first blush, the sentence sounded insensitive. Upon reflection, it was not. It was just the damn truth. As Margot gave Owen a hug and her best wishes for the days ahead, she took a deep breath and decided to do her best to move on. After finding Carol, they decided it was time to move on.

There was little talk in the car ride home, but Margot graciously thanked Carol for the ride. Once inside the house, she poured herself a glass of Rose wine and agreed with Owen that no one lives forever.

# CHAPTER 13

# *Flowers for Carol.*

MARGOT VISITED HER FAVORITE GREENHOUSE AND FOUND Frank, the owner, in the front watering some tulips. "Wow, even the owner has to do some grunt work," she exclaimed.

"Oh, I don't call it grunt work," Frank answered. "Fact is, I enjoy caring for the plants as much as paying the bills."

"I can relate to that," she answered.

"Margot, I haven't seen you in a few weeks. Is everything OK?"

"Some good. Some bad," she answered. "The high points were that I went to London to visit my daughter, and even visited Kew Gardens."

"That's a beautiful place."

"Stunning," she answered. "I also went to the New York Botanical Garden. and may even take a class or two there."

"What kind of class?"

"Landscape Design looked fun," she answered.

"It is," he answered. "But I don't think you really need it. From my exposure to you, you seem to already know which plants are to be planted when and where.

You also seem to have an good instinct of which plants go well together…both in terms of height and bloom time."

"I'm flattered," she blushed.

"Hell, you could probably run this place as well as I could. What other kind of classes do they offer?"

47

"They have one called Therapeutic Horticulture, which intrigues me," she answered.

"I don't know what that is." "Wow, you think that would be fun?" he asked.

"Maybe, I'll bet it's also geared for people who may be thinking of a mid-life career change."

"Maybe I should take that class," Frank laughed. "Although at 79, I am a little beyond mid-life…but occasionally, I do wonder about what's next."

"So do I," Margot admitted.

"But you already have a great job," Frank said.

"Yes, on paper. But I've been doing the same thing for about 30 years. After a while, everyone needs a change."

"I know the feeling," he answered. "But don't do anything rash. Hell, you could always come and take over this place. You know as much about gardening as I do."

"Hardly."

"Well, it doesn't take that long to learn."

There was a little bit of an awkward pause. After a few moments, Margot smelled the tulips that Frank had been watering. "These red and pink ones look and smell great. I think I will take 3 or 4 pots of them. No, make it 5 or six. I want to bring a few to my next door neighbor, Carol.

"As you know, it's a great gift," Frank smiled and helped her bring the pots to the checkout counter. "Any kind of special event?"

"No, hardly. One of our female neighbors died of cancer, and friend Carol drove me back and forth to the funeral parlor. I just want to say thanks."

"Sorry to hear that," Frank reacted.

"Was she old?"

"Not really. She was only in her mid-forties." Margot answered.

"Damn." Frank reacted. "Well, no one lives forever."

"Funny, that's exactly what her son in his 20's said to me near the casket." Margot agreed.

"Well, it's true," Frank nodded. " Maybe I should be thinking about that myself."

Margot just smiled and answered. "Please, Frank, stop.."

After accepting her payment, he walked her to her car carrying many of the tulips. "A few of these may cheer your neighbor Carol up….and she will definitely appreciate them. Tell her how to care for them….since I believe you definitely know the ins and outs of flower care."

"You are too nice," Margot answered, and waved goodbye.

That evening, Margot brought 3 of the tulips to her neighbor Carol and thanked her again for the ride back and forth to the funeral parlor. Carol was very appreciative of the generosity, and gave Margot a hug for her thoughtfulness.

# CHAPTER 14

## *Another chance for Silver Singles.*

AFTER HER INITIAL EXPERIENCE ON THE SILVER Singles 50 year plus dating site, she was doubtful that she would ever try it again. However, she had not explicitly cancelled the service. Perhaps the frequent inquiries and photos from men her age helped cheer an otherwise ordinary day.

She was also semi-inspired by her daughter's new fresh start…and her ability to juggle two boyfriends. The other factor was that axiom about "No one lives forever" that she had heard twice in one week.

This man had written to her via email twice. Unlike her first Silver Singles experience with a man who was occupationally too close for comfort, Wayne had changed careers about 5 years ago. He had been a dentist for 25 years, until he completely changed course and now owned a kennel where he raised dogs and even boarded them when his customers would go on vacation. He lived in the rather affluent village of Bronxville and looked attractive enough for a hello. On a "What the heck" whim, Margot responded and wondered if he cared to get a cup of coffee one day.

Yesterday, he answered back with a phone call. "I know this is short notice, but I wondered if you might want to get a quick bite, a coffee or a cocktail Sunday afternoon at Anthony's restaurant in Elmsford. No pressure."

"I like the sound of that." she retorted.

"How about 1 p.m.?"

"I'm game if you are," Margot said, and after providing her address and exchanging a few more pleasantries, hung up.

"Nahh, I have a Toyota Rav 4 to transport the dogs around… but your instinct is right. It does smell like dogs inside that vehicle. "

"Well, I am glad you picked me up in this Buick," she chuckled..

Unlike her first experience at Silver Singles, it was more fun and more enlightening. When Wayne brought her home and walked her to the door, she said thanks, and gave him a kiss on the cheek.

She didn't know if she would see him again. Somehow, she thought she

"I like the sound of that." she retorted.

"How about 1 p.m.?"

"I'm game if you are," Margot said, and after providing her address and exchanging a few more pleasantries, hung up.

After watching the Sunday news, she watered all the plants and put on a nice casual outfit. A few minutes before 1 p.m., Wayne knocked on the door and was quite handsome in real life.

"Nice neighborhood," he exclaimed. "Nice house, too. Smells good in here, too, Is that your perfume?"

"No, It's probably the fresh tulips. I got them yesterday and just watered them."

"Well, they are very fragrant."

"Would you like a cup of coffee before we go?" she asked.

"Mmmm, tempting…but maybe we should just get one at the restaurant." he suggested.

Margot shook her head yes, exited her home and got in his Buick. "I thought it might smell like dogs, given your current occupation, " she giggled.

On their journey to the restaurant, they each covered off some background information. Wayne explained that he had been divorced for 7 years now, and had one son who now lived in St. Louis, Missouri. According to him, it had been an amicable divorce after a twenty-year marriage.

By contrast, Margot told him that her husband had died about five years ago, and his daughter now lived in London. "As a matter of fact, I went and visited her a couple weeks ago." She offered.

"How long had it been?" he asked.

"A few years, but it was great fun to be together…and I'm not going to wait so long until we can get together again."

"That's good advice for me and my son in the Midwest," he nodded in agreement.

When they arrived at the restaurant, the two of them entered and were escorted to a table near the window. Wayne ordered a glass of wine, and asked Margot if she would like one, as well. She smiled, and ordered a glass of Rose.

After the toast, Margot was interested in quizzing Wayne about his career.

"But it sounds like you basically liked the profession. Why did you want to leave it?"

Wayne shrugged. "I had done it for more than 20 years, and felt I had learned all there was to learn in the dental field. Besides, after my wife left me and son moved to St. Louis, I was lonely. I always liked dogs. They keep me company, even when they howl at night. During the day, I give them walks, and always feel refreshed when doing it." change. "I'll bet being a dentist was a tough life. A lot of pain." she said.

"Not really," he chuckled. "See, the patient is the one in pain, not the dentist.

It was always my job to ease or eliminate the pain. Not just that. I often was also charged with teeth cleaning , so I could make my patient's smile bright and sunny…..so they could look like a move star. Besides, it paid well."

"That's what I have found out first hand as a patient," she agreed.

"Ever think of changing careers?" Wayne asked innocently.

After a long sip of her rose, Margot nodded yes. "Wayne, is it difficult to do so might. when you are a success in your chosen profession?"

"In a word, yes," Wayne answered. "It's a big adjustment. Your decades long regime is all shook up. And no matter how much you think you know about the new mystery field…there is so still so much to learn. But it's worth it, especially if you feel you have out-lasted profession #1. At least, that has been my experience."

Margot and Wayne enjoyed the coffee, which had just been served. "What would you do if you moved beyond banking?" he asked.

"I might go into gardening," she quietly admitted for the first time. "Of course, it doesn't pay as well."

Wayne laughed at her last thought. "That's not the point. You think scooping up dog poop and brushing airdales pays better than administering root canal? But it does give me a chance to reinvent my life."

"You're a good man, Wayne."

"I try to be."

Unlike her first experience at Silver Singles, it was more fun and more enlightening. When Wayne brought her home and walked her to the door, she said thanks, and gave him a kiss on the cheek.

She didn't know if she would see him again. Somehow, she thought she might. But as she reminded herself, it was a first time get-together. No one really knows beyond tomorrow.

# CHAPTER 15

# *Back at the Bank.*

IT WAS ANOTHER TYPICAL WEEK AT CITIBANK. The bulk of Margot's days was balancing the books for clients who had questions. As the most senior person at the Hastings branch, she also opened up many checking accounts and savings accounts for customers.

There were a few high points of the week.

A relatively new customer named Julie McKinnon had ambitions to own her own business. She was in her early thirties and had been a physical therapist at Dobbs P.T. for the past ten years. In her meeting with Margo, she told the banker that she had a loyal clientele, and recently had ambitions to start her own Physical Therapy firm.

"How long have you had these dreams?" Margot asked.

"Maybe a year." Julie answered.

"Have you checked open spaces where you might be able to set up a practice?" the banker asked.

"I've just begun to see some places."

"I wouldn't look for a place right down the street from your current employer," Margot suggested. "That might backfire in this small town."

"Actually, I found a place in the next village," Julie retorted. "I don't want there to be any hard feeling with my present employer, who has treated me well. "

"Probably a good idea."

"The places I have looked at are about $6000 a month. Do I have a good enough record here at Citibank to swing that?"

Margot looked at her folder. She had always paid her bills on time, but didn't have a huge savings account. "We might be able to arrange that for you, as long as it doesn't go a lot higher or require a lot of equipment."

"Minimal equipment," Julie nodded. Then she stood up and shook Margot's hand. "Thanks for the advice. I will keep you posted."

"Good luck, Julie."

Margot's next act of personal assistance came towards the end of the week. It was not a happy experience.

A regular customer named James Anderson asked to have a private meeting with her. When he entered her office, he looked glum, but took a seat across the dress and nodded at Margot. "I have bad news," he began.

"What's the problem?" she asked.

"My wife and I are getting divorced and I need to check my savings," he said.

"Oh, I am sorry to hear that," she said. "How long have you been married?"

"Twelve years," he answered.

"Any kids?"

"Two....she will probably gain custody. Can you give me an idea of how much I will need to surrender?"

"Well, divorces are not cheap," Margot acknowledged. "Given the length of time you have been together, I would think it could be 50/50.

"Damn," he reacted. "I have one more question for you. Here's what I have been wondering. Do you think I could move some of my money from Citi into another account...under a different name? Perhaps I could open a new account under my middle names— Edward David—and move some of my savings there. That way I could hide some of my hard-earned savings."

After of moment of letting this sink in, Margot just stared at him and answered. "I can't do that. It's against the law. Besides, your wife will probably need the money as much as you do."

"I was afraid that's what you would say," Mr. Anderson answered. "OK, it will probably be 50/50. And then there will be childcare. And then there will be legal fees."

"Do you have a lawyer?"

"Just got one," he answered. He advised about the same in terms of 50/50 numbers." After a pause, he shrugged. "OK, so be it."

Margot nodded again sympathetically. She then watched him exit her office and the building…and then shook her head in sadness.

There was one highpoint towards the end of the week. She got a call from Cliff, telling her that he was going to have three art pieces exhibited in Manhattan.

"Wow, that was quick," she said.

"Thanks to you," he answered.

He told her the address of the gallery and the Sunday hours of the grand opening.

"I would definitely like to see the show," she said.

"That would be great." he grinned. "See you there."

As she hung up, she was proud of his accomplishments, and of the encouragement she had given him.

# CHAPTER 16

## *Cliff's art show.*

I T WAS A BEAUTIFUL SUNDAY MORNING, AND Margot secretly wondered if she was so smart to give up her sunny March day. However, Cliff's enthusiasm about his first big art exhibition was enticing…and besides, she had promised.

The Grimandi Gallery was in the West Eighties on a beautiful block with restaurants and a few other shops….and then there was that one art gallery where Cliff had his art debut. After parking around the corner, she walked down the street and entered the gallery, which was about half-filled with people.

As soon as she entered the place, Cliff walked over to greet her and introduced his wife, Betty. She smiled broadly and shook Margot's hand. "I have

heard such good things about you. For one thing, you encouraged my husband. And also, you made the finances happen for the two of us. I want you to know, Cliff has never been happier, and neither have I."

"Oh. that's so nice to hear," Margot responded.

"It's a beautiful gallery, isn't it?" Cliff asked the banker.

"Yes, and I am so happy for you."

"Over here at the counter here, we have some snacks, sodas, coffee, and wines," he showed the way. "Why don't you grab a bite and a drink first. I am talking to a possible customer, but there are tables outside…and I'll come and get you as soon as I am through."

"Take your time," Margot advised, and filled a small plate with cheese, crackers, and cup of coffee. She took a table outside and enjoyed the bright sunshine.

After about ten minutes, Cliff and his wife came to the table and escort her inside the gallery.

"I have three pieces here and they are all in the same style," Cliff admitted.

They are all fairly realistic watercolors…with a twist. I like to create art that has an immediate impact and a residual mental tickle. So often I use words with my art.

I create a list on a theme and then paint and image over it. C'mon, let me show you an example."

He then led her to a piece which he called "Jacks." The main visual was a large silver Jack next to a red rubber ball and several small jacks. This was painted over a list of words:

Jack of all trades. Jack Benny. Jack London.

Jack Nicholson. Jack Russell. Jack Kennedy.

Jack Jones. Jack & the Beanstalk. Jack Daniels…..and perhaps 30 others.

"Wow, that's clever," Margot reacted. "And the art is really cool."

"You like it?" Betty asked.

"I definitely do."

Cliff smiled. "People here seem to appreciate it. Let me show you another piece." He then walked her to another piece. The main visual was a cowboy on a horse. Again, it was dramatic and realistic. It was painted over another list:

Hopalong Cassidy. Tom Mix. Gene Autrey. Chuck Conners.

Lone Ranger. Marsall Dillon. Ben Cartright. Lash Larue.

Roy Rogers. The Cisco Kid. Butch Cassidy. Wyatt Earp…and dozens of others.

"Let me guess," Margot smiled. "Cowboys. "

"Exactly!" Cliff responded. "One more," He then showed her a slightly more mysterious piece. The main visual was a series of bright orange orchids blooming out of fresh white snow. Against this, there was yet again another list:

Richard Branson and other late bloomers. Albert Einstein.

Martha Stewart. Meryl Streep. Colonel Harland Sanders. Sylvester Stallone. Vaclev Havel. Alan Rickman. Roget. Winston Churchill. James Micheneer. Nina Zagat.

And dozens of others who made it big beyond their 20's.

After staring at the piece for many minutes. Margot was nodding her head. "Late Bloomers!"

"You like it?" Cliff asked.

"I absolutely love it," she responded. "It talks to people my age. I want to buy it. I really do."

"You don't have to do that." Cliff responded. "I'm just glad you came and saw my work.

"I really want it, "Margot insisted, and walked to the cashier to complete the purchase.

"You really don't have to buy it." he answered.

"Hey, I love it. I want it." Margot answered, and only at the check-out did she discover it was $1500…which she thought was a fair price for a piece of art so intriguing.

"It couldn't have happened without you," Cliff repeated and his wife Betty raised glass to salute Margot.

"I am so happy I came," the banker said. "I plan to hang it above my dining room table so I can be inspired every day." She then raised a glass to the happy couple. "I am so glad this worked out so well. All my best to both of you."

Afterwards, she shared another coffee with Cliff and Betty outside and was so complimentary of Cliff's fresh start. She then left the gallery with a rejuvenated pep in her step.

# CHAPTER 17

# *NYBG classes*

IT WAS ABSOLUTELY INSPIRING TO SEE HOW happy Cliff was reinventing his life in his mid-fifties as an artist. Margot didn't know Cliff's wife well, but had to admit that even she was beaming with her husband's new career.

Obviously, it didn't pay as well as owning a big, successful car dealership in White Plains. Having helped with his financial loans and balance sheets, she knew the figures…but that was not the point. He had earned hundreds of thousands of dollars in the past few decades (and saved a lot). Even with modest investments, it was probably enough to afford plenty of watercolor paints and winter vacations in Florida.

The look of freedom on Cliff and Betty's faces was inspirational.

Is it possible to feel that way each and every day? Margot wondered. True, she had high points in her banking life when she assisted people. At this point in her life, the goal of feeling satisfied on a more regular basis, struck her as a worthy goal. Ah, but where and how to achieve that?

After her visit to the art gallery, Margot reviewed the catalogues she had kept from the New York Botanical Gardens. She had loved gardening for dozens of years, and felt like investigating whether it might provide a more satisfying career path.

One program that attracted her was the curriculum called landscape design. It moved well beyond plant science, but she did honestly believe that an intro class on this subject could be a useful background. It involved learning about different plant groups—flowering plants, conifers, ferns, bushes and trees. Truth be told, she knew most of these things from years in the garden. But she believed it would be a good start, so she signed up for a weekend class. Without trying to brag, she thought it was easy.

The next class was not such a layup. It was called therapeutic horticulture. It truly was geared to older adults. In fact, Margot was the youngest one in the class. Many of her classmates were from assisted living homes, day care programs, skilled nursing, and memory care facilities. The goal was to brighten the day of those who have physical, sensory, cognitive, psychological, and social aspects of aging.

Ironically, Margot found the class a miracle. By the end of the lecture, most of the students had a brighter countenance. Many of them liked the aroma of the flowers. Even more were mentally lifted by replanting a flower, and sharing the accomplishment with a fellow classmate.

A few weeks later, she signed up for another class that addressed the horticultural advantages of addressing trauma. There were people in the class that had suddenly lost a spouse, and were finding it difficult to recover. Others had their own traumas. One young man had been in involved in a auto accident and had both legs amputated. An older woman in class had been shot in a grocery store by a mass event that just happened months ago. It can be a lingering effect, and horticulture can lift one's spirits.

Margot agreed, and told the class that she had always had an interest in gardening. "As a matter of fact, every time a flower blooms, I feel fresh and renewed."

In this class, they learned how to feed several plants, flowers and small trees…even from a wheelchair. Not surprisingly, a tip was to supply just the right amount of water. You should not drown the plant, or deprive it of moisture a few killer.

One older woman in class who was walking with two canes particularly appreciated this class. She explained that she was in a wheelchair until a month ago. Fortunately, she improved physically…. but was still mentally and psychologically stifled. "This class is a real upper," she exclaimed to her fellow students.

People wondered what Margot's trauma was. She explained that by comparison, hers was relatively minor. She had lost her husband and her daughter lived far away in London. The bigger trauma these days was that she had reached a point in her life where the sameness of work was depressing her, and she admitted she was just in a tizzy trying to figure out what was next.

The instructor in the class explained that trauma does not have to be outwardly evident By and large, all the classes at NYBG enlightened Margot. Generally, she liked her fellow students and even kept in touch with some of them. She also truly appreciated the curriculum and felt she was learning new things. Many of the people in class told Margot that her insights were helpful. Some even suggested she should do this for a living.

On the last day of her vacation, she took a trip to her favorite nursery to buy some fresh flowers. When she was looking at the houseplants, Frank approached her.

"Welcome back, Margot, I haven't seen you for a few weeks." he said.

"I know, I took a few weeks off from work."

"Well, I hope it was fun."

"It definitely was. I even took some of those classes at the Botanical Garden.

One was on landscape design…and a few were on therapeutic horticulture."

"Oh, yeah, you told me about those classes. Why those? You seem healthy enough."

"I am, but I thought it was extremely interesting to see how flowers can cheer the soul of even those who are afflicted with pain."

"Maybe I could use some of those therapeutic insights," he responded with some sadness in his voice.

"What do you mean?"

"I went to my doctor last week, because I felt that at age 79 (I'm turning 80 next week)..at this point, I thought I I should maybe slow down a bit. Unfortunately, he told me, I definitely should…since the tests show that I have early form of cancer."

"Oh, no….I'm so sorry to hear that," Margot said, and hugged his arm.

"What kind of cancer?" she reluctantly asked.

"Pancreatic," he quietly said.

"Damn," she added. She knew of Pancreatic Cancer since her older brother died of it. It's a ugly disease that often limits your lifetime dramatically.

"Yeah, so if you don't see me around the place, it's because I am going to have to go in and out of the hospital a lot." came to say hello.

"I am so, so sorry," Margot said sympathetically.

"Yeah, and I believe I should probably sell this place, even though it will break my heart."

"No," she instantly reacted.

"It's time," he said with a tear in his eye. "I just need to know how to figure out a way to do it."

"Do you have a bank?" Margot asked.

"Yes, the Citibank in Hastings," he said.

"No kidding! I work there, and am in charge of all customers who want to buy or sell properties, or businesses. I don't think I have ever seen you in the bank."

"Probably not," he agreed. "I do almost all my banking and saving needs by mail or by computer. In the upcoming days, it will probably be more visible in the bank. . Besides, my right hand man, Bernie, drives there once a week to make my cash deposits from our customers who make transactions in that way."

"That's probably a good plan, especially under the circumstances," she answered. "But if you ever need any special attention, come into the bank and ask for me. I'm in a private office across from all the tellers."

I will do that," he answered.

"Can you do me a favor?" she asked. "Do you have any idea how much money greenhouses like yours sell for?

"I have a rough idea, since I know a few other greenhouse owners that have sold their places in the past few years. Of course, all greenhouses are different…"

It's a tough problem for me. I want the Westchester Greenhouse to strive and survive…even me."

"That's a noble thought," Margot said. "Even so, it's a good idea to talk to a real estate agent just to get a ballpark idea of the price. Don't sign anything yet. Come talk to me first. I may have an idea or two about how you can achieve what you wish for in the days ahead."

"I don't know exactly what the Westchester Greenhouse is worth. The greenhouse itself is probably half an acre. From my research, it's probably worth $200-250,000 dollars. The plants inside are probably worth another $150,000. The property is probably an acre and a half. The price of that? I don't know. "

"That alone could be worth a million," Margot guessed.

"Wow," Frank reacted.

"Yeah. See. Westchester property is pretty expensive."

"That's why you need to talk to a real estate broker."

"I will, but I really don't want to," Frank answered. "I'm afraid the real estate agent will find some asshole from New York City who wants to tear down the greenhouse and build a mansion of a second home for himself. If only for the sake of my customers and my employees, I want the Greenhouse to strive and survive…even me." "Are there any of your employees who could conceivably buy the place?" she "Sadly, no." Frank answered. They are great people, but they don't have that kind of money."

"Do they know about your condition?"

"Many do. I'm afraid to dwell on it with them. They are almost like family," he answered sadly.

Margot then ventured into personal territory. "Do you have a wife? Kids?"

Frank shrugged. I had one wife, but she died thirty years ago. I do have one son who simply wants to sail boats in Hawaii."

"I see, Margot answered sympathetically. "Perhaps that's why you should at least meet with a real estate agent."

"I will," Frank answered. "I have to go to the hospital over the next few days. But I'll try to have a real estate agent come by and just give me an estimated price. Hell, maybe I could even sell him a pot of orchids or something."

"If so, I am sure it would make his day," she did her best to smile. "Keep in touch. Don't sign anything. If you get an estimated price, come back and see me next Monday."

"See you at 9," he answered. "Want me to help you carry your plants to the cash register."

"I think I can manage," she said, and gave him a hug before paying and exiting the place. When she got home, she planted her new flowers, and looked forward to seeing him again.

# CHAPTER 18

# *Margot prepares for Frank meeting*

IN ADVANCE OF HER MEETING WITH FRANK, she looked at his file from the Citibank vault. From the looks of his balance sheet, he lived conservatively in Dobbs Ferry. The house appeared to be quite nice, and was completely paid for thirty-five years ago. According to the records, there were no requests for refinancing or home improvement loans.

In so many ways, he was an ideal Citibank client—a long-term guy who posed no alarm bells or question marks about his ability to continue this relationship in good standing.

Promptly at 9 a.m., Frank entered the bank and asked to speak with Margot. Seeing him enter the place, she came to greet him and escort him to her office. "Coffee," she asked.

"That would be great," he answered, and she called for her secretary to bring two cups.

Once he took a sip, she asked how he felt.

"I feel the same every day now," he admitted. "My legs are bad. I can barely walk around the greenhouse, and—this may be too personal—I also have bladder problems so I have to wear man diapers these days."

"Damn, what do the doctors say?"

"They say the chances of surviving one year are slim."

"Ouch," she reacted, feeling his pain.

Intent on changing the subject, Frank spoke. "I did call a real estate agent as you suggested. I was able to get Lisa Carroll from Houlihan-Lawrence to come to the place and give me an idea of a property price."

"And…"Margot probed.

"She walked through the greenhouse and the grounds, and looked at my balance sheets of P&L over the past several years."

"You had those? " Margot asked.

"I always need them for taxes," he answered. He then pushed forward. "She suggested that the whole thing could probably be worth about $1.5 to $1.6 million dollars. "She also told me that if she handled the deal, she would want about 8% of the asking price."

"That's about what it is up here with real estate people. Sometimes, you can reduce it down to 5%…but not much lower."

Frank then sighed. "I asked her if she could restrict possible buyers only to those who would want to keep the Westchester Greenhouse continue as is…with the same employees."

Margot anticipated the answer by shaking her head no.

"You are correct, Margot. My real estate gal said that's impossible, "In fact, she laughed at the very thought of it. She explained that a potential buyer had the freedom to do anything with the property. He or she could turn it into a yoga spa,, or grocery store, or an office space…or anything."

"That's the law," Margot agreed.

"And that's what scares me. I don't want to see my life-long pursuit transformed into a 9-5 office space."

"Nor do I." Margot agreed. She then pulled out a folder and took a minute to go over the figures. "I've had a busy week, too," she told him.

"Here's a surprise for you, Frank." she ventured beyond her private thinking. "I might be interested in buying the Greenhouse from you."

Despite the fact that he had seen her in his business many times over the years, the thought did jolt his head. "You want to buy the place?"

"Maybe so," she answered.

Again, Frank took a pause. "It's not a part time job."

"I realize that. I would quit my job at the bank, and devote all my energies to the Westchester Greenhouse."

"Are you serious?" he asked with some hope in his voice.

"Yes."

"But you have a great job at the bank." he answered.

"It's a good job…but I have done it for many decades. And at a certain point, it became the same old thing…over and over again. I'm at the point in my life where I truly need a career change. As you might know from my frequent visits, I love the gardening business. I love your greenhouse. I love the sight of a fresh blossom and the smell of every single flower. I feel rejuvenated by it…and the very idea that I could help other people enjoy that same emotion truly excites me."

After a few seconds, Frank responded. "I thought it was just a serious hobby for you."

"That's the way it started," she admitted. "But with my classes at the New York Botanical Garden, I have begun to feel it is much, much more."

"Would you keep it as the Westchester Greenhouse?" he asked.

"Yes."

"Would you retain the staff?" he also asked.

"Yes."

After a pause, he ventured into uncomfortable financial territory. "Do you have the money to make such a deal?" he wondered outloud.

"I believe so," she answered. "For one thing, I have been a top executive of the bank for more than 30 years. They pay a decent wage. My husband was a lawyer who made a good living, and left the bulk of his savings to me. My house is paid for. My only daughter has good job and is financially on her own. Of course, it depends on what your asking price to me may be."

"I'll tell you. $1.5 million." He instantly answered.

She grinned. "And better yet, we could dispense with the real estate agent fee…and you could keep that money. Between your lawyer and my lawyer, we could seal the deal."

"Wow, I could not be happier," Frank said.

"Me too," Megan agreed. "But let's talk to our lawyers, and figure out next steps. Do me a favor. Don't talk to your employees about this. I agree they are good people. If this all goes through, I would like us to have a meeting to explain it all to them. And just so you know, I will need at least a month to untangle myself from Citibank and the staff here."

"I totally understand." he nodded. After a pause, he continued. "To be perfectly honest, I knew you loved this gardening business…but I would have never predicted that you would want to enter it full time."

"I have been privately thinking about it for many years." she admitted.

"Well, if this all goes though, I am glad that it will benefit Westchester Greenhouse and all my valuable employees."

"I repeat this, Frank. I will keep it as your beloved Greenhouse. And will keep all your employees…provided they would want to stay."

"They would. They know you."

After a few minute pause from each party to let this transition sink it, both of them stood up and shook hands. To further cement the deal, Frank gave Margot a big hug, and said "Thank you…for everything."

"And thank you back," she answered. "Let's talk to our lawyers and keep in touch before too many weeks go by."

"Agreed," Frank agreed and, even though he had a stiff leg, seemed to skip out of the bank with new vigor.

# CHAPTER 19

# *The Waiting Game.*

OVER THE NEXT FEW WEEKS, BOTH MARGOT and Frank did their best to retain contact with their lawyers, and go about the day to day of their businesses.

For Frank, it was iffy. If you know anyone who has had pancreatic cancer, it is a rather consuming illness. For one thing, there are frequent MRI's and Pet Scans to see if the cancer has spread (which is inevitable). Beyond that, there is the psychological tailspin that accompanies the disease.

Beyond that, Frank did his best to attend to his greenhouse, water some plants and act busy a few days a week and put on a happy face. It barely convinced his employees…but they totally respected the man, knew better than to pry into to stage of his fatal cancer.

Margot, on the other hand, did her best to clean up her paperwork at Citibank without alerting any alarm bells. She did schedule a meeting with her young assistant and asked to know how he was doing at Citibank. She had also arranged a raise for Brian, since she wanted some continuity of loyalty from him at the banking firm.

Other than that, let me explain something. She didn't really hate her job. It was not an ugly existence. Often, she felt she had helped people….but not often enough to make her smile. It was just too many decades of doing the same old thing….and wearing fancy business clothes to do so.

After two weeks and many discussions with her late husband's law firm, she learned that such a transaction with Westchester Greenhouse was well within her savings. if needed, she could borrow more.

Meanwhile, Frank privately checked his friends in the greenhouse business about the proposed sale, and given the circumstances, they approved. She told Frank that she trusted him and moved forward.

Actually, she considered calling her dear daughter Annie in London to ask advice before moving forward. However, upon reflection, she had signed nothing. Also, Annie had not really asked her approval before changing jobs. Consequently, she opted to keep it quiet until it was finalized. Privately, at Citibank, she asked trusted advisors if she could borrow a half a million for an investment if needed. They gladly approved and frankly told her that she reminded herself that every person's life belongs to that person. No one else can live your life. No one else can truly advise you about what your next steps should be.

Within a week, she had heard from her lawyer and so had Frank. Also, both lawyers had spoken with each other, and everything seemed to be moving along swimmingly.

Satisfied that it was really going to happen, Margot talked with her real estate friends to see if Lisa Carroll's asking price was relatively accurate. While they all did operate in rather wealthy Westchester County, they all thought it was more than fair.

When he explained his situation to his long-time lawyer, Mr. Attorney suggested he might actually be able to gain more. "Put it on the market. Make the interested parties bid against each other. You may be able to get hundreds of thousands of dollars more."

Frank gently rejected the advice. He told his attorney that he respected the bidder from Citibank, wanted to accept it, and would like to know the next steps…and also how long it would take. Answer: about 3 weeks.

Margot had to the same vague timetable from her lawyer. After one more conversation with Frank to ascertain the details and seriousness of his decision to management of Citibank and offered her resignation. She gave two weeks notice, and began to tell the people in the office, who could barely believe that she would no longer be there after that date.

She called Frank and invited him to her Citibank office on her last day with the lawyers. She knew there would be forms to sign and notary public stamps to exchange.

After so many years, it was a bit of a sad day for Margot, but also a liberating day. Many of her co-workers were crying and blowing kisses to one of their very favorite employees.

Once all the papers were signed, Frank and Margot shook hands with the lawyers and headed out the door. They both agreed they would go to Westchester Greenhouse and Frank would explain the upcoming transition and introduce Margot. She couldn't wait.

# Chapter 20

## *The Greenhouse Announcement.*

That night, Frank emailed all his employees and asked them all to get there at 8.30 a.m. promptly—a full half-hour before the doors open for customers. He teased that it was an important meeting, and that he would have fresh coffee for everyone.

He got there at 8:00 and put on a fresh pot of coffee. As it perked, there were lots of whispers among his employees. In total, there were about 16 workers. About eight of them worked the floor helping customers and replanting flowers during the day. The other eight had heavy lifting. They would carry the bushes and trees to the right spots, and unload them from trucks.

At 8:30, Margot entered the facility, carrying her own cup of coffee from home. Once Frank saw her, he waved, and began addressing his employees.

"Hello, everyone," he began. "You are probably wondering why I asked you all to get here a half hour early on a Saturday. I will tell you." He then took a gulp of his own coffee cup. "Perhaps most of you have noticed that I have been missing days and feeling ill during many of the days. The reason is simple: I have cancer, and it's not a good one. As a matter of fact, I have pancreatic cancer, which is usually fatal. "

There was a murmer from the crowd of employees. Fact is, many of the workers had begun to suspect something was wrong with their owner and friend.

Frank continued: "So I reached the conclusion a few months ago, that this couldn't go on forever…although I wish it could. I talked with a real estate person to discover the prospects of selling the place. It was possible. But what was not possible was that this place could automatically continue as Westchester Greenhouse, and all of you would have a job and a future here. Hell, for all I knew, someone would want to buy the place, level the greenhouses, fire all of you, and turn it into big apartment complex. That's not what I wanted. After building this place and working so hard…no way.

Many of you know Margot. She has been a regular customer of Westchester Greenery for many years. And she knows a lot about gardening. Not only from here, but she has taken many professional classes at the New York Botanical Garden.

"But guess what? She was also my banker. And when I explained my situation to her, she offered to buy the place. She promised to keep it a greenhouse…and even more important, she promised to keep all of you employees in place .

"I said she was also my banker. As of 5 p.m., yesterday, she ceased to be a banker, and become the owner of Westchester Greenhouse. So say hello to your new boss. This is been a good business for many decades, I wished for it to continue, and feel that all of you could have a good future here."

"My wishes came true when I talked with Margot Roberts. Margot, raise your hand."

There was applause from the group and also some relief that they would still have their jobs during this transition. As this occurred, Margot went to front of group, grabbed his hand and they raised hands together as if they were all winners.

"Now, a few other things," Frank spoke again. "I want you all to promise me a few things. I want you all to work your butts off and not ask Margot for a raise, at least for six months or a year. Let her get her feet wet with all the ins and outs of this nursery. Now, as for me…I will still be around as long as I can. I will have to see the doctors a couple times a week, and maybe more as the weeks go on. But I will be here to help as much as I can, as long as I can." He then took a deep sigh, and looked at Margot. "Margot, would you like to say a few words?"

She shook her said yes, and looked at the crowd. "I want you all to know that this is a dream come true for me. I had worked at Citibank for more than 30 years, and began to desperately feel I needed a change. My favorite field is gardening, and my favorite place is Westchester Greenhouse.

"I would also like to thank Frank for his decades of service here. He has built a great business which serves so many people well in the community. I simply want I simply want to keep it growing in the right direction. I will be here every day…or at least as many days as I can each week. And Frank, please come here as often as possible, as long as your health permits.

"As Frank said, I have been coming here for many years, and recognize many of you. I would ask all of you to schedule a half hour or so with me in the next weeks or month and explain what you like to do most, and any ways you think we can improve the nursery. OK, gang , let's raise our coffee cups and give a nice round of applause to Frank, "

Not surprisingly, the crowd did just that. Many of the workers had worked with Frank for more than a decade. Everyone came up to give Frank a pat on the back, and shake hands with their new boss, Margot.

After a few minutes, Frank looked at his watch and said, "Wow, it's almost 9 a.m. Time to open the doors and help the customers. Margot, should we all get to work?"

She took the cue and told the group, "OK, let's all get to work."

With that, the crowd went to their usual stations and prepared for a busy day to keep it growing in the right direction Then Frank motioned for Margot to follow him into his small office, where he had two chairs, a desk and a storage cabinet.

"I think that went well," Frank said.

"I agree," Margot responded. "I think some of the people were sad, but that's to be expected."

After taking a deep breath in his office, the two of them looked at each other and smiled. Frank then stood up. "If it's OK, we'll walk around the nursery, and say hi to folks. I will introduce you to some of the more regular customers who do their flower shopping here.

At this early hour, there were only a few customers. In advance, Frank said that if he didn't know their names, it meant that they were not significant, regular, big-spending customers. As they walked through the aisles, he simply said a friendly "Hi" to these folks. If they looked back at Margot, she did the same, "Hi there."

Within the next ten minutes, the twosome ran across a thirty-something who was shopping for pansies. She was a familiar face to Frank.

"Diana, are you finding everything you need?" Frank asked.

"I think so," the customer answered.

"Diana is one of best, regular customers, Margot. I always do my best to make sure gets everything she needs. And Diana, I want to introduce you to Margot. The new owner of the place. I'm getting to the age when I need to back off a bit…and she's a very knowledgable good soul.

"Wow," the young customer said and shook Margot's hand. "Good luck.."

"Margot, welcome aboard. If there's anything I can explain when Frank isn't here, just ask."

I'm sure I will." Margot answered.

"Everyday, at the end of the day, Jenny puts all the receipts and the cash in my office. She is amazingly reliable and trustworthy."

"Thanks, Frank," she answered. "And good luck." She then winked at both of them and made sure her cash register was ready for the day's business.

At the same time, Margot and Frank cruised the premises.

After a few minutes. Margot asked a key question. "You don't tell your customers about your condition.

"No, I only want them to find happiness here in the greenhouse," he answered with a smile.

After a lunch, Frank and Margot resumed the route. They said hello to customers who liked indoor plants, outdoor plants, shrubs and small trees. Most of them were happy with the introduction of Margot, and appreciative of all that Frank had done for them throughout the years. Not surprisingly, a few of them were concerned about Frank, and wanted to know what he would be doing in the years ahead. Frank always answered as cheerfully as possible. As he had earlier told Margot, he was not prone to discuss his cancer with regular customers. Instead, he simply answered that it was time to enjoy some other things.

"OK, Understood," Margot answered, and felt so bad for Frank and his condition. She also appreciated all he was doing to keep his workers in line, and his customers optimistic about their gardening futures.

The couple continued their walk. As they did so, they inevitably said hi to some of their employees in an individual way. At the cash register, Frank introduced Margot to the chief cashier, Jenny.

"Jenny, I am sure you recognize Margot."

"Yes, I have seen her many, many times," Jenny answered. "By now, I probably know your credit card by heart."

"I'll bet you do," Margot laughed. "Please don't spend it on anything frivolous."

"Is a dress from Saks Fifth Avenue frivolous?" she giggled.

"Maybe, but you don't need that." Margot replied. "You look beautiful as is."

About a half hour later, they ran into Louis, who was looking at the forsythia in the bush section. As Frank had learned over the past years, Louis, who was 40-something, who liked to do his own shopping, and often bought quite a lot. As they approached, Frank asked this regular customer if he was finding everything he was looking for

"Definitely," Louis answered.

"Louis, I would like to introduce you to Margot."

"A new employee?" the customer asked.

"Not exactly," Frank answered. "The new owner."

Margot then extended her hand and said hello.

Louis answered "Well, good. I'll be seeing you here then."

"Yes,," she answered. "Need any help"

"Nah, Todd over there will help me bring these up the cash register. But for now, I'm fine."

"Good." "Good." "Have a nice day." Frank and Margot said and exited the scene. "He's a man of few words," Frank admitted when they were out of earshot.

Many of the customers were quick hello's and goodbye's. There was one regular customer who wished to know more. Her name was Claudia, a woman in her late forties, who definitely appreciated Frank, but also wanted to know Margot's background and ability to run this beloved greenhouse.

Frank answered first. "Allow me to vouch for Margot. She has been a regular customer for many, many years, and knows her way around the garden. She is also a smart businesswoman and has taken many professional classes at the New York Botanical Gardens.'

Margot was more explicit. She told Claudia she had worked in a bank more than 30 years, and for many years felt that she needed something more fulfilling and enriching. She always loved gardening….and in discussions with Frank, felt that this was the right place. "It's a wonderful nursery," she added. And I hope you will feel the same way for many years."

"Omigod," Claudia said after a pause. "I can definitely relate to your story, Margot. At my age, I feel exactly the same way, having worked in the computer field for 30 years,..and lately, more and more, I feel I need to recreate my life."

"I know the feeling," Margot agreed

"I'm not so sure what I want to pursue though," Claudia said. "It could be health care. It could be home decorating, I don't know. Meanwhile, I keep coming to this nursery, and every time, I buy a plant and see it grow, I feel renewed."

"I know the feeling," Margot repeated.

"Obviously, I will keep coming here," Claudia said. "Someday, we will talk more at length about this crossroads since you have already experienced it and moved forward. I could learn from you. Congratulations."

"Thank you," Margot answered.

"And congratulations to you too , Frank for your decision to move forward in your own way."

"I hope to, and that's a good thing, Claudia," he said.

It was her high point of the afternoon. She loved the environment. It was so enriching to see people feeling new life with their purchases. It felt good to be on her feet and meet strangers in that pursuit.

At the end of the day, she gave Frank a big hug for her unforgettable morning and her memorable afternoon of meeting customers. In some ways, it was a plant business. As she learned during the day, it was also a people business.

At the end of the day, they walked back to their business office, and met Jenny, the chief cashier who was bringing a bag of cash and credit card receipts to the file cabinet.

"Was it a good day?" Frank instinctively asked.

"A better than good day," Jenny answered. "After all, it's that time of year. Everyone wants the sight, the smell, the rejuvenation of fresh life in their home, their front yard, and their back yard."

"You bet," Margot reacted.

"OK, I am out of here. Will I see you both tomorrow?" she innocently asked

"I'll be here," Frank answered.

"Absolutely," Margot redoubled.

With that, Jenny left the office and slowly walked to her car. Instinctively, she believed and hoped that the greenery would survive and maybe even thrive for the years ahead.

# CHAPTER 21

# *Hello, Annie.*

AFTER HER FIRST FULL DAY AS THE owner of Westchester Nursery, Margot could barely wait to share the news with her daughter. Given the time difference she woke up early enough to reach Annie in the London morning.

After a few minutes of chitchat, Margot got the point. "I have some big news, Annie. " she announced.

"Oh, do tell," the daughter pleaded.

"I left me job at the bank," Margot proudly said.

"No."

"Yes, For several years now, I feel like I've just been doing the same old, same old. I've been going to this greenhouse for years, and lately I've been taking classes at the New York Botanical Garden.. The owner and I talked. He was at the point in his life when he wanted to sell it….and I was at the point of my life when I thought it would be fun to buy it. So I did! So now I am the owner of the Westchester Greenhouse!"

"Is that the one you used to take me?" Annie asked.

"Yep."

"It's a beautiful place. I remember it."

It's great." Margot answered. "I no longer sit behind a desk all day long. I walk around. It's outdoors. I see people smiling, smelling, and buying their favorite plants. It's wonderful!"

"Wow, mom, you sound so energized." Annie admitted. "Even my friend Adam remarked to me that you sounded very happy walking through Kew Gardens when you were here."

"I was," Margot declared. "My place can't compare with Kew Gardens, but it is beautiful in its own right. And it contains everything a gardener needs. Also, the staff seems very nice. I met them all yesterday, when Frank, who owned the place introduced me to everyone."

"That's great. So out of curiosity, what is Frank the owner going to do?"

After a pause, Margot answered. "Well, he's 80 and has a bad cancer…so he will have to spend a fair amount of time with the doctors. But he told me and the staff he will come to place as long as he's feeling OK."

"Well, I am sorry to hear about his condition, mom," Annie said sympathetically. "But it sounds like he will do his best to create a good transition for everyone."

"Exactly."

"And mom, you sound better than I have heard you in years."

"I feel better. It's a nice place to spend the day. And a good service that I can provide to all the people in the community."

"Wow. Big News," Annie responded.

"Yep. And dear Annie, you sort of inspired me, changing your job. You sounded happy with your move….and I thought I should make myself happier, too. But honey, right now, I have to get to work. I just wanted you to know before too many days elapsed."

"Thanks, mom," Annie answered.

"Gotta go, Love you dear Annie," Margot said.

"Love you back," And with that, both of them hung up smiled.

When Margot arrived at the nursery, she instantly felt a surge of revitalization. Frank was already there and suggested that they continue the meet and greet that they had started yesterday.

They walked through several of the less busy aisles and said hi to several of the employees who were busy tidying up the rows of flowers and plants.

Once in the main greenhouse, they cheerfully greeted Jenny, the chief cashier, who happily waved back. Just a few feet from her was a young man of about 30, who looked busy organizing things by the cash register.

"Wait right here," Frank told Margot. "I want to introduce you to Bernie, who has for several years been my right hand man." He then called out Bernie's name and asked the young man to join them away from the cash register. "Bernie, you were here for yesterday morning's meeting, were you not?"

"Indeed I was," Bernie answered. "Frank, I am sorry to hear about your medical condition. And Margot, I wish you all the best here at Westchester Greenhouse. I intend to do my best to help you in any way I can."

Margot extended her hand and shook the hand of the young man. "Thanks, Bernie."

"Bernie has been at the nursery for four or five years," Frank said. " He knows how the place works and quite honestly, I think of him as my assistant. "In fact, when I have had doctor appointments, I call him at home the night before just to make sure he can be there to make sure things run smoothly the next day."

"That's sweet, Frank." Bernie responded. "It has been a pleasure."

"You should have each other's numbers," Frank continued. "Margot, if you need a day off—and you might sometime in the heat of summer—I suggest you call Bernie to make sure he is at the nursery the next day. And Bernie—if you need a day off—I hope you call Margot to let her know. That way, our bases are always covered."

"I definitely will," Bernie answered.

"And I will too," Margot agreed, glad to have a reliable second in command.

Once Frank and Margot got back to his small office, she said she enjoyed meeting Bernie.

"He's a great guy," Frank said.

"Did it occur to you that maybe he should take over the nursery?"

"Quite honestly yes,… but I knew he didn't have anything close to the money required. In fact, his parents are poor and he drives an eight-year old car that always needs repairs." He then wrote down the young man's number and gave it to Margot, who put it in her purse. "I'll make sure he has your home number too. He's very reliable."

'Thanks," she answered. After a pause, she asked Frank. "Just out of curiosity, how often do employees take days off?

"Well, during the summer months, we are open every day…. and everyone needs a breather, at least a couple days a week for their own sanity. Of course, I will be taking more days off with my ill-ness….but Margot, you will want to take a few days off every week just to keep that smile on your face. And Bernie's the guy to call when you need break."

"Good to hear," she responded.

After lunch, the two of them went back into the crowded nurs-ery and said hello to some of the regular customers. They all seemed to be happy to be there, and had few questions.

One woman in particular piqued Margot's interest. Her name was Roz and she appeared to be in her late 40's. Once she heard Margot's history, she gave her a hug and said she could definitely relate. Evidently, Roz was a school teacher who had worked at the same grade school for more than thirty years, until she began writing books a few years ago. "But she was a great customer all those years, "Frank said. "Like you, Margot."

"Yeah, the gardening kept me sane,"

"I know the feeling," Margot responded.

"And the new job keeps me happy," Roz said. "One day, we'll have to compare notes on our transitions,"

"Glad to," Margot answered. "Did you find everything you were looking for?"

"I always do," Roz said and wished Margot all the best.

In the late afternoon, Frank and Margot retired to the office. Frank admitted that he would have to be at the doctor's office a few days the following week—Wednesday and Thursday. "I already told Bernie, but I realize I should also always tell you."

"Probablyagoodidea,"sheanswered."Howareyoufeelingthesedays?"

"Just so-so." he admitted. "That's why I have to visit my cancer doctor a few times next week. But quite honestly, I do feel better every day that you are here."

"That is very nice of you," Margot answered.

After putting the day's earnings in the file cabinet, the two of them closed up the place and walked to their respective cars.

Once home, Margot made a light meal and sat at her dining table. She looked at the painting above the table called "Late Bloomers." As she enjoyed her rebirth, she felt good reminding herself that she was not alone in this desire to regenerate one's life in mid-career.

# CHAPTER 22

# *Slow Monday.*

A s Frank had predicted, Mondays were a little slow at the Greenhouse. It was a good time for him and Margot to sit at the desk and go over some of the things he had in the file cabinet.

In one large envelope, he had all the cash and credit card receipts for the week, as compiled by Jenny. As usual, she had tallied the totals…which he was now happy to share with the new owner.

"Not bad for one week," she acknowledged.

"It's usually good this time of year. And usually, Bernie brings all this to the bank and deposits it. As you can tell, they have been my most trusted, valuable employees. Just so you know, I gave them both a nice raise before the sale went through…so you won't have to worry about them for some time."

"They both seem like great employees."

"My favorites," Frank agreed. "And speaking of employees, let me take you through the staff—their start dates, salaries, and principle responsibilities."

She perused the list for several minutes. "Seems like a good crew…and it seems like they all get along."

"They do," Frank agreed. "I wish they all felt more like a team, but maybe you can help expedite that with some get-togethers."

"I think that would be good for them…and for me." she said. "How long do most of the staff workers stay with the nursery?"

"I probably lose maybe one employee a year. Not bad…but you always have to keep your eyes and ears open for new prospects. Lots of the workers have friends who would like to work here."

"That's good." She said.

"Now let me go over our list of suppliers, when they come, what they supply and when they like to be paid."

"Wow, you are organized," she complimented him. "You should work at a bank."

"Well, I promised you this would not be a financial nightmare," he answered.

In the afternoon, Frank and Margot did walk the premises and say hi to a few customers. It felt good to spread the cheer and freshness of the plants all around them.

Tuesday and Wednesday were the first days in which Margot was on her own as the head person of the nursery. A few suppliers made deliveries, and as instructed, they presented their bills to Bernie, who put them in the file cabinet and alerted Margot that they generally liked to be paid by the end of the month.

"Do they generally expect a tip?" she asked.

"Not normally." Bernie answered. "Frank usually simply gives them all a Christmas gift."

Margot did spend time with each of the employees, and did her best to get to know them all better. A few were university graduates. Most simply had a year or two in college. Some still attended a few times a week. They all seemed to get along.

Occasionally, Bernie would introduce her to a client who was a regular.

One was a 50ish woman named Linda. Looking at the tulip plants, Margot saw his signal and introduced herself to the woman. "Welcome," she said. "If there's any way we can help, just let us know." The two woman spoke and compared their background information

For the first 25 years of her life, Linda had been a stay-at-home mom. She explained that her husband had died, and her kids had all graduated and moved to other parts of the country. "It was lonely for several years," Linda admitted, "but I started coming to the nursery to feel renewed. And then I got a job as a real estate agent.

I found the flowers from the Greenhouse very useful. I plant arrogant blooms in display houses to make them feel more like a home. I find that if a customer entered the place and got a whiff of fresh flowers, they are more apt to be want to buy."

"Wow, that's amazing," Margot responded. "Do you have a card."

"Of course," Linda responded. "Are you looking for a new home?"

"No, but I find a customer who is, I will refer them to you. The real reason I want your number is that I am finding so many people in mid-life who find live plants such a plus. At some point, I may want to get you all together and compare notes about starting a second career."

"That sounds fun," Linda remarked. "Definitely include me."

"I will," Margot promised and helped carry the fragrant tulips to Jenny at the cash register.

# CHAPTER 23

## *Frank slows down.*

OVER THE NEXT SEVERAL WEEKS, THE WESTCHESTER Greenhouse adjusted rather easily to the transition of new ownership. By now, it was the height of summer and all the plants and bushes required more water. The staff kept them healthy with all the nutrients they needed.

Not surprisingly, the place was busy on the weekends. It also had a fair amount of people on the weekdays.

Frank continued to introduce Margot to many of the regular customers.

However, his health had begun to diminish and he only came to the nursery a few times a week, usually on those slower weekdays. If the greenhouse suppliers came in on those days, he made sure to introduce them to the new owner and frequently praised her. As usual, if he was at the doctor's, Bernie did a great job making sure that Margot knew all the important people who came to the nursery—be they customers or suppliers.

After several weeks, she called Cliff the artist to see how he was doing in his new chosen profession and invite him to her new place of business.

"You quit the bank?" he said with some surprise. "You were so good in that job."

"Yeah, but I did it for almost 30 years. Same old. Same old. Like you, I needed a fresh start, so I bought the Westchester Nursery."

"Wow, that's where I got the flowers that I used in that painting "Late Bloomers.""

"I love it and look at it every night. It hangs on the wall in my living room." she answered.

"That's great. You took an instant liking to it."

"I wonder if you have any prints of that piece of art?" Margot asked.

"I have two or three," he answered.

"Can you run off more?" Margot asked.

"How Many"

"Maybe 10. No, make that 15."

"You want to hang one in every room of the house?" Cliff teased.

"No, I meet a lot of people here who are going through mid-life career changes…and I think that's an inspirational painting."

After a short pause, the artist answered, "That's so flattering, I actually have a print of that piece hanging in my house. But I will run off more. It will take a few weeks. You don't need them all framed, do you?"

"No, just the artwork. Wait a minute, maybe you should frame one, and I'll hang it here in the nursery."

"Wow, that's great. When I get it framed, I will come and visit you at the nursery. When I get them, I will bring them all to the Greenhouse. I'll call first and make sure you are there."

"I will most likely be there, since this is the busy season…but yes, call first, just in case."

After a moment, Cliff added, "Margot, you sound great in this new job."

"As do you," she responded. "Hope to see you soon."

Over the next several weeks, Margot devoted herself to caring for the plants and her employees. Even Frank had to admit that things were working well, and complimented Margot on the transition.

"I got lucky in finding the right person to take over this place," he told her one day.

"Lucky for both us," she agreed.

"When I am here, I sometimes walk the aisles and say hi to the staff. They all feel very good about you being in charge."

"I am doing my best," she humbly answered.

"Well, it seems to be working. "

On one of the afternoons when Frank was at the greenhouse, Cliff came to place with framed print of "Late Bloomers." He had called earlier and talked with a staff member, who answered, "Yes, of course, Margot is here,"

"Knock, knock," he said outside the office of the Westchester Greenhouse management.

Margot motioned for Frank to just stay in his seat and opened the door.

"Cliff! Wow, I am so happy to see you," she said.

"I have the first print beautifully framed," he bragged.

Margot walked him over the desk and introduced the artist to the elder statesman of the Westchester Greenhouse. "Frank, I'd like you to meet Cliff—an amazing artist. When I was a banker, I helped convince him that a new mid-life career was possible for him. I went to his first art show in Manhattan and saw this piece of art and immediately bought it. It spoke to me."

"That's what art is supposed to do," Cliff smiled.

"Cliff, this is Frank, who owned this place for many decades and helped build it to the success it is today. Eventually, the time came when he wanted to sell it…and I was a more than willing buyer. See, I took your example, Cliff. that a new career mid-life is a beautiful thing.

While the two men shook hands. Margot opened the package and saw the print of "Late Bloomers."

"Omigod it's beautiful," she exclaimed.

After a moment of looking at it, Frank gushed. "I absolutely love it. Hey, that's fine art."

"Would you mind if I hung it in this office?" she asked.

"It would definitely bring beauty to the file cabinets, desk and chair." he said with a sense of humor.

"The other prints will probably take another week," Cliff admitted.

"That's OK. Just bring them in when you've got them." she said and walked Cliff out of the office into the rows of flowers.

"So how is the new career going?" she asked.

"I couldn't be happier," he answered.

"I am so happy for you. By the way, the reason I want extra prints is that I meet many customers here at the nursery and I would like them to feel inspired in starting a new career….like you were, and I am. I am thinking of calling them all together one afternoon and rewarding them with a print of "Late Bloomers." I'll let you know when it's happening.

"That's wonderful.," he added.

"Would you like to attend? If so, I will invite you."

"I would be flattered if you did," he quickly added.

In the ensuing weeks, Cluff made sure he had plenty of prints for the attendees.

# CHAPTER 24

## *The late bloomers meet.*

ON ONE OF THOSE DAYS WHEN BERNIE visited the office to drop off some bills from suppliers, he saw the piece of art on the wall.

"Hey, that's great," he freely announced to Margot, who was sitting at the desk. He looked at it long and hard, and turned his head to his new boss, smiling.

"Amazing," he looked at her with thumbs up "It's what we do."

"Have a seat." she invited him to hear her thoughts. She explained that she was thinking of starting a support group for people who are trying to feel refreshed, like a perennial plant does every year."

"That's a great idea," he agreed. "I have met so many people here at the Greenhouse who are trying to find exactly that—a way to restart their lives. Many of them are in mid-life….30's. 40's, 50's… and it's a difficult leap. They come here to remind them how plants restart their lives. "

"Right," she added. "So I am thinking of having a group of our customers meet here one evening and discuss what they are going through."

About three weeks later, on a Wednesday night after the Greenhouse had officially closed, more than a dozen invited people showed up in the main greenhouse for a thing called "Late Bloomers" — with a sign to direct them to the when we are venturing into the great unknown." As requested, Bernie had prepared chairs and a perennial on each chair for anyone who attended.

Frank walked to the center of the small meeting room and waved to all the people who were seated in their chairs. "First of all, I want to thank you all for being such valuable customers throughout all these year. I think I introduced most of you to Margot, a friend who bought the place and has every intention of moving it forward. Margot, the meeting is yours." He said and sat down to applause.

Margot took the stage. "From my dear Frank, and my most valuable employee Bernie, I learned that everyone who is here is about to start the second (and perhaps most exciting halves) of their lives.

"It's a daunting challenge. I know, having done this," Margot said. "And I have met so many people in the past few years who have also gone through the same transition. My greatest wish? You share your experience with the other people who have come here tonight to give them hope that what's ahead may be just as promising or maybe more so than the years you have already lived,."

"If it makes you feel more relaxed I will tell you my story. I was a bigwig at a bank for 30 years, but got bored with the job in the last 10 years or so. I loved going to the nursery and planting new flowers in and outside the house

"After more than three decades in the banking business, I decided to bite bullet, and make a change…after all, life's too short. So I ended up buying this place and creating a new life. Any of you have a journey to share on the subject of rejuvenation?"

The woman named Roz was the first to raise her hand. " I can relate the idea of reinventing one's life. I had been a grade school teacher for decades. A good job, but deep down, I always wanted to write childen's books. I'm trying. Maybe I'll get one done soon."

"Linda explained that she was a stay-at-home mom for 25 years and had recently decided to become a real estate agent. She said you felt rejuvenated every time she put a beautiful plant in all her homes for sale."

A man in his 50's explained that he had been in the army for 30 years, and left with PTSD. He said he was looking forward to becoming an Uber driver with a fresh flower in a vase in the front seat.

A woman told the crowd that she had been a legal assistant for 25 years and was thinking about becoming a travel agent.

A long time waitress was thinking of joining the network news.

One after another. All different dreams. All new hopes.

After the group had told their stories, Margot called on one more person. "Cliff, come up here and explain your journey."

Cliff walked to the front of the room and explained that he had run an auto dealership for decades. "It was a big, successful business…but at a certain point, it didn't make me happy. I wanted to paint pictures. So with the help of Margot, I decided to pursue my passion. I just recently had my first art show in Manhattan. "

Margot stood next to him. " In fact, I loved one of his paintings so much that I bought one. "

"I find it inspirational for reinventing one's life….so I asked him to run off prints for each of you. While the prints were being distributed, Cliff explained that he started with the words—a list of people who found their greatest success in in their 30's, 40's. 50's and beyond. Over that, he painted lilies growing out of the snow.

Everyone in the crowd applauded again.

Linda in the crowd raised her hand. "I found this meeting inspirational. Do you think we could have another one?"

"Yes, we could probably do it again. Maybe next month." After a minute, she "I hope you can make the next one," she said. Frank agreed. "By the way, I have a cousin who runs a greenhouse in Stamford, Connecticut. I may tell him about this. If he's interested, could you run a similar meeting in Stamford? "continued. "However, you only get one painting. If you bring a friend, let us know in advance and I'll have Cliff run off a few extra prints,"

Frank took center stage, He said, "I think it would be great to keep the momentum going." While Bernie was pouring coffee for everyone, the crowd just lingered and chatted with each other. After about fifteen minutes, they left and effusively said thanks to Margot, Frank, and Bernie.

Once they were all out the door, Frank turned to Margot and gave her a hug. "That was a magnificent meeting," he raved. "I have never been prouder of the Westchester Greenhouse."

# CHAPTER 25

## *The Late Bloomers meet again.*

DURING THE WEEK, FRANK, MARGOT, AND BERNIE saw many of the attendees from the meeting many times buying many things—plants, flowers, shrubs. They all said they thoroughly enjoyed the meeting, and several said they planned to invite a friend or neighbor who was going through a similar transition.

At their next "Late Bloomers" meeting, Frank gushed about how happy he was to see so many of them in the nursery after the last meeting. "I guess a fresh idea on our part can actually generate business. So thank you all," and now let me introduce the brain of this initiative, Margot,"

Margot took the stage and was almost speechless from Frank's generous accolades. After discussing the subject matter of the meeting, Margot explained that rejuvenating one's life at mid-point it similar to plants that re-bloom after many years. She once again explained her journey and asked others if they had a similar experience.

Claudia raised her hand and with a smile told the group that she had just quit her job as a computer wiz, and thanks to the encouragement of one of the attendees, enrolled in health care classes.

One new attendee raised her hand. "I've been a secretary for more than 25 years and would like to explore something more fulfilling than typing letters. I've thought of becoming an airline employee or a baker."

A carpenter hoped to become a firefighter for his local department.

A librarian admitted she had just quit her job to write novels.

An electrician hoped to audition as a singer.

On and on. It was exciting to hear everyone's hidden ambition. And not surprisingly, Margot brought the idea back to perennials on the chairs, "Perhaps they can demonstrate to you the idea to come back again year after year, despite changes in the environment."

"Also, as a momento of your attendance tonight, I am giving all the new people here an artistic print of a man who attended last week, who gave up a lucrative car dealership to create art for a living. This one is called "Late Bloomers, and I hope it inspires all our new members here."

Bernie then distributed the new prints to all the new attendees.

The next hand in the air came from a young man in the second row.

"Hi, my name is name is Joey, and I had been a barber for about thirty years.

I did it on the side for many years…but after having many editorials published in the Westchester Journal, and many pictures published in that newspaper and many others, the Westchester Journal offered me a job. A dream come true. I wonder if I could get some pictures and cover this meeting for the newspaper."

Margot looked at the group who seemed to gesture that it' was OK with them.

"And good luck at your new job with the Westchester Journal., she added.

As happened in the last meeting, the crowd valued the one-on-one conversations with attendees who had gone through similar life-changing decisions. As this time, Joey the photographer was busy snapping photos of the attendees.

As a writer, he also questioned people about their impressions of such a lesson. All of them were so grateful, since it came with no strings attached. In fact, it came with a gift every time they attended. Most of them gushed about the Westchester Greenhouse's leadership in addressing this issue.

# CHAPTER 26

## *A newspaper breakthrough.*

ON PAGE 3 OF THE WESTCHESTER JOURNAL, Joey Bova had his first big feature story replete with pictures. The headline was: "Is there a chance for a fresh life after many years on earth? A nursery has the answer." The pictures were flattering.

One was a picture of Margot with two attendees holding plant gifts. The other was a large shot of the art work "Late Bloomers."

According to the article, "Last Wednesday, Westchester Greenhouse gave many of their middle-aged, regular customers an inspiration about regenerating their own lives. The comparison they drew was from their own gardens—where many plants come back year after year, despite inevitable changes in the environment. Perhaps the more obvious analogy was to the late blooming plants—such as chrysanthemums, which were given as a gift to each attendee."

"Margot Roberts, the mid-fifties new owner of Westchester Greenhouse and brainchild of the seminars explained that she was a late bloomer—like those plants you have in your hand. She had been a successful banker for about thirty years, but wanted a fresh start away from the desk as a nursery worker. She claimed to be renewed every day."

"Invited customers in the crowd joined in. Some has successful careers for many decades before making the change. Others were still thinking of changing careers in mid-life, and seemed encouraged by the approval of the crowd.

"One woman named Claudia told me that she had quit her job as a librarian, and was now studying to be a health care worker. She said, "Enough being surrounded by books inside all day. Now I can help people personally, often with walks outside…surrounded by plants.

"The attendees were also given the gift of art—a limited edition art print by a man named Cliff Carlson, who had been a car dealer for many decades, until he decided to devote himself to his real passion—art. Recently, he participated in an exhibition in Manhattan, and Margot fell in love with one of his paintings. It's called "Late Bloomers," and features the names of many people who became famous in mid-life, overpainted by a fresh orchid in the snow.

"All in all, it's a wonderful way to spend a late afternoon. According to statistics, the nursery has hit a trend that has grown in last several decades. True, young people in their twenties and thirties have always changed jobs many times. But more and more people are now actually changing careers in mid-life. Approximately half of all workers consider it…and according to statistics, 88% of them are happy they did so.

"Most people, like me, consider it a great, satisfying leap forward. These seminars by the Westechester Greenhouse encourage those who are sitting on the fence. The get-togethers are open to their regular customers…so if you're on the fence. It might be worth visiting a few times, and buying some late-blooming perennials just to remind you of the possibilities in life beyond the here and now."

By Thursday, many people came to the Greenhouse and brought along the news article by Joey Bova. "Did you see this?" customer after customer asked Diana at the check-out lane.

Many customers presented it to Margot who was in aisles, always trying to meet new people. Everyone seemed proud to be buying their plants at such a progressive nursery.

Frank was ticked with the news coverage and particularly proud that he had passed the baton to such a visionary leader. He also faxed the news story to his cousin Charlie Claggett, who ran a similar nursery in Stamford, Connecticut.

Charlie had talked with Frank about importing the idea to his Greenhouse, and was impressed with the news coverage. "Maybe I should invite my local newspaper to cover the event." he suggested.

"Probably not a bad idea," Frank agreed. "Just make sure they credit her as the originator of the idea."

"Don't worry. I'm not trying to steal her." Charlie chuckled.

"Have you set up a date yet?" Frank wondered outloud.

"I was thinking in a couple of weeks, maybe Friday after the greenhouse closes…but I want to clear it with Margot."

"Probably a good idea." Frank remarked. "I've been sick, but if I can make it, I'd love to come and say hi to my cousin."

"I would love to see you," Charlie encouraged him, and that afternoon went back to trying to clear his calendar for the event.

On the Friday afternoon of the event, Charlie had assembled about fifteen of around the nursery. It was similar to the Westchester Greenhouse, but perhaps a little more upscale…as were the customers. Many of the men wore ties and many of the women wore dresses.

Once inside the meeting room, they gathered with Charlie and Paul Konowitch, a writer/photographer for the Stamford Sentinel, who had been invited by Charlie. Before the event started, he asked for a shot of the principles—Charlie, Frank, and Margot, each holding a small potted plant of Blue Moon Wisteria. After a few shots, he motioned to the trio that he was happy with the result.

Within ten minutes. it was time to start addressing the crowd. Charlie took a hand mike and welcomed the crowd. He explained that they were there because they were regular, valuable customers… and perhaps they were at an age when they might be considering a mid-life career change. In truth, he knew that some of them had recently achieved this leap, and that the others might be considering it. He explained that he had invited a writer/photographer from the local newspaper, but would respect anyone's privacy if they wished.

He then referenced his cousin Frank, who ran the Westchester Greenhouse and introduced Margot. She quickly explained her journey from bank office at Citibank to owner of the Westchester nursery. She also explained that she had run a few of these seminars, given the inevitable link to flowering plants that are late bloomers to human beings who like to come to life after their early days in the marketplace.

When she opened the discussion to the group, she was impressed with the openness of the participants.

There was a 40-something maid that had just decided to go back to school to get a degree in public relations.

A middle-aged pharmacist admitted he was interested in becoming a landscape designer.

A fifty-something accountant told the group that after a few decades "of feeling stuck" in the same day-to-day, she had just physical therapist.

And on and on. As had happened in Westchester, some of the attendees called out advice for those who honestly confessed to feeling trapped in a mid-life job, Others offered congratulations for their honesty.

When the seminar felt that it had run its course, Margot again made the connection to plant life, …."especially those late-bloomers available here at the beautiful Stamford Greenhouse. And speaking of late-bloomers, thanks to Charlie, we have a beautiful art print from my friend Cliff that celebrates "Late Bloomers."

Here they are. Everyone gets one, even Paul from the local newspaper. Enjoy!

And if you ever feel stuck, take a look at the piece, and remind yourself that re-birth is always possible." As she handed them out, there was a growing crescendo of applause.

Charlie thanked his loyal customers for attending, and closed out the meeting.

Within the next few days, there was wonderful article in the Stamford Sentinel. It captured the enthusiasm of the meeting and featured two photographs – one featuring Charlie, the owner, his cousin Frank, and Margot, who was clearly identified as the owner of the Westchester Greenhouse.

As it turned out, there were many letters to the editor about the burning topic of a mid-life career change. Given the interest, the newspaper actually published an editorial a few weeks later, addressing the topic and encouraging people in their 40's. 50's and 60's that their best working days may still be ahead.

Charlie thanked Frank for the tip on this seminar, and admitted that his business soared given the publicity. He wondered if he could spread the word to some friends of his who owned some greenhouses in Boston and Providence. Rhode Island.

"I guess so," Frank responded, "As long as the Westchester Greenhouse and Margot gain credit for initiating the idea."

"I'm sure that would happen." Charlie assured him.

And so, the momentum for the "Late Bloomers" idea began to expand.

"Over the last week, I have been in demand in Boston, Rhode Island, and New Hampshire. I assume they will also have raves."

"Omigod," her daughter Annie answered. "Mom, I always knew you were destined for big success. Let me figure out the next steps to fame on Google."

"I appreciate that, and you have been a godsend in my life," he began "But I think I am close to the end."

"Well, you never know," she retorted.

"Yes, I do," he answered abruptly. "I want you to know what pleasure the Westchester Greenhouse has brought to my life. Yes, my marriage was a thrill while "That's not the purpose of the call, " Margot retorted. "I just wanted to keep you posted on my progress."

# CHAPTER 27

## *Annie is so proud of her mom.*

On the heels of Margot's successful seminar in Stamford, Charlie called a few of his greenhouse buddies in New England and spread the word.

Of course, the timing was tricky, but Margot worked a deal with the suggested greenhouses in Boston and Rhode Island. With Bernie's help, she was able to find some slower days in October, Each time, it was a huge success with great news stories in the local newspapers.

On one brighr and sunny October Saturday, Margot called her dear daughter. After about ten minutes hearing about dear Annie's happiness in her new job at Google. ("it's fascinating. I learn something new every day. I think they like me there. I am so glad I made the change."

"And you mom, any good news?" Annie probed.

"You're not going to believe what a news hero I have become," she began. "I have run this seminar on Late Bloomers at my new Greenhouse, but then it expanded to Stamford. Each time, there is positive publicity."

"Over the last week, I have been in demand in Boston, Rhode Island, and New Hampshire. I assume they will also have raves."

"Omigod," her daughter Annie answered. "Mom, I always knew you were destined for big success. Let me figure out the next steps to fame on Google." she responded.

"Well, you never know," she retorted.

"Yes, I do," mom answered abruptly. "this endeavor of yours seems to catch on wherever it plays."

"It seems to," Margot agreed.

"Hooray hoory for mom. You are destined to be famous,"

"No, stop. Applause is not the purpose of the call, " Margot retorted. "I just wanted to keep you posted on my progress."

"I love it. Send me the news stories. Keep me posted. Meanwhile, know I love you."

Once back and the greenhouse, she wanted to thank Bernie for all his extra efforts. Once she was alone with him in her office, she ventured into an area that Frank had cautioned the employees to avoid. "I'd like to speak to you about your salary," she said. "In view of your amazing contributions to this place, I'd like to raise you 20%."

"Omigod," Bernie exclaimed.

"I couldn't do this place without you. I value you. And I want to make it worth your while,"

"You do every day," he smiled. "But the raise would be very much appreciated.

"I will make it go into affect next week," she promised.

"Thank you, thank you, thank you," he gushed.

# Chapter 28

## *Frank gets sicker.*

THE NEXT WEEK, FRANK'S CONDITION TOOK A turn for the worse. As a patient of Memorial Sloan Kettering in New York City, he had suffered for the last few month, but been treated as humanely as possible. However, in the past ten days, he became weaker and weaker. On Wednesday, he was checked into critical care. Margot visited as soon as she could, during the hospital visiting hours. As he reminisced about his life, he admitted loving his dear wife while it lasted "…and I still love my son, but I never hear from him. So for the longest time, That Greenhouse has been my life."

"And what a good life it has been," she answered.

"Yes, most days. I love my customers. And as you have captured in your seminars, I love the smell and revitalization of plant life. Year…after year…after year. It has always cheered me, and I will miss it. "But I am so amazingly proud to have passed the torch to you before I die. You make the Westchester Greenhouse new again, and proud again."

"You built the place, and made it great," she countered. "And I am going to say a prayer that you can come back again."

"Prayers are good, but it's tough to face the final days," he admitted. Margot asked if there was something to do or someone she should reach.

"I have my son's number in my address book. He never calls… but if you reach him, that would be good."

After a few minutes of silence, Margot gave him a kiss on the cheek and exited, She got the son's name and number and called him that night. To her amazement, she was able to connect with the guy.

"Scott, this is Margot Roberts, and I am a good friend of your father Frank…who is very, very sick."

"I think he told me some months back that he had some kind of cancer,"

"That's true. It's pancreatic…and it has become much worse, As a matter fact, I think he may pass away in the next day or two. I just wanted to alert you, since I know you are a long way away in Hawaii. Maybe you could clear your schedule and come here to New York? "

"Well. Wow….that would be tough. Your name is Margot?" he asked. "Do you go out with him?"

"No, no, no," Margot corrected him. "I bought his beloved greenhouse when the doctors advised him to sell. I just thought you might like to visit him and tell how much he has meant to you. I am sure you would do it in a sensitive way."

"Let me write down your name and number," Scott said. "I'll see what I can do with my schedule."

"That's good," Margot responded and gave him the contact details. "And I'll get back to you if things change. Meanwhile, say a prayer for your dad…and try to come see him in New York."

"I'll see what I can do," he answered. "Thanks for the info…but I have to go now."

"OK, Goodbye." After she hung up, Margot just sat there for several minutes shaking her head, and thankful that her one daughter was more sensitive.

# CHAPTER 29

# *Goodbye Frank.*

THE NEXT DAY, SHE CAME TO THE nursery at the usual morning hour. When she encountered Bernie and Diane, she decided it was best to share the sad news of Frank's deteriorating condition. Both were devastated, and wondered whether they should visit the hospital.

"Quite honestly, he looks awful," Margot answered, "and he has tubes all over his body. I think it might be best to think of him in his better days." Both completely agreed.

Later in the day, Margot called the hospital and reached the attending nurse.

"How is Frank?" she innocently asked.

"Are you Margot?" the nurse asked. "Frank mentioned you a few times and wanted us to know that you are an important person in his life."

Sensing the runaraound, Margot asked her original question. "How is he?"

The nurse quietly answered. "Unfortunately, Frank passed away about ten minutes ago. He was in bad shape and in pain, and considering his condition….it was inevitable."

"Omigod," Margot instinctively reacted. "What do I do next?"

The nurse became more businesslike. "You should notify his lawyer. Hopefully, he had a will."

"I'm sure he did."

"And then you should contact his favorite funeral parlor. They will pick him up, and help handle obituaries, schedule, and the nature of the services."

"Wow, I will do my best, This may take me a day or two." Margot pleaded.

"That's OK…but if it takes much longer, you should let me know."

"I definitely will." Margot answered and hung up, thankful that she had a daughter who was more caring than Scott.

Over the next few days, she arranged things with Frank's lawyer, who she remembered from their sale transaction. She assumed that he had access to his estate for any of the expenses ahead. She did ask him if Frank had expressed any preference for wake and burial services. The lawyer respectfully answered no, but suggested that she handle it, since his son Scott was always so difficult to reach.

Her next call went to Edwards-Dowdle funeral parlor in Dobbs Ferry.

In their time together, Frank had mentioned this as good place a few times, In talking with Larry, the funeral director, she learned that they could arrange for pick-up from the hospital, preparation, obituary, the wake and burial. It would cost some money, but Margot correctly assumed that Frank's law firm could assist in this. Also, she recalled that he did have an account at Citibank, and Bernie had access to it.

In talking with the funeral parlor, she asked if the wake could be several days from now on a Monday, so she could alert all her employees and do her best to reach Scott.

After trying to reach Frank's son for several hours, she finally did succeed in contacting him. He admitted it would be difficult to get from Hawaii to New York over the next three days, but would do his best to be there. Margot gave him the address and phone number of the funeral parlor just to make sure he had the appropriate information.

She then reached Bernie and informed him of the sad news. Bernie suggested that when she came to the nursery, she should call the entire staff together and make the announcement. She agreed.

On that afternoon, she asked for a meeting with all employees at the close of the business day. The word had begun to spread, and all of the staff was crestfallen.

She explained that he had passed away in the morning, and that in her conversations with him, he was always the proudest of the greenhouse and all the employees.

A few of the workers had questions.

"In view of the fact that it's a Monday wake, and our slowest day of the week, don't you think we should close the nursery that day?" Jenny asked. "I hadn't thought of it, but I think that's a great idea," Margot answered.

"I will get a photo of him and words "In memorium" to announce it on the front gate." Bernie volunteered. "If you'd like, I'll also help the funeral parlor write an obituary for the newspaper."

"That's great." Margot responded.

"One more thing," Bernie added. "I've been to that cemetery and they do a fine job with flowers, but I think I should bring some of Frank's favorite flowers from the nursery as well."

"Good idea," Margot said.

A few other employees shared some reminiscences about Frank and cried.

"If you'd like," Jenny added, "Maybe Bernie and I should call our most regular customers and let them know when the wake is.I think they would like to attend."

"And I'll call our suppliers and his cousin in Stamford, " Bernie added. "A lot of the greenhouse owners in the region knew Frank and respected him."

After a pause, Margot said, "We will all miss him. I plan to say some words at the funeral parlor. If any of you have any other anecdotes, let me know."

They all shook their head. Many of them hugged each other. Silently, they all left the Greenhouse that evening.

On Monday morning about 7:15, Margot received a call from Frank's son, Scott. "What time is the service? How long will it run?" he asked.

"It will be all day today, until about 9 p.m." she answered.

"I'll be there about 2 p.m. Long flights from Hawaii and Los Angeles."

"Would you like to say a few words at the funeral parlor," Margot asked.

"No, that's not necessary." he answered.

After a pause, she said, "Well, I am sure your dad would be impressed that you made the trip to pay your respects. The burial is the next morning," she added.

After a sigh, Scott said, "Oh, I can't do that. I have a late night flight back to the West Coast after tonight."

"O.K., O.K." she said. "Good of you to come"

At the end of this short conversation, she shook her head again in disbelief, but quickly got dressed to be at Edwards-Dowdle funeral home. When she arrived, she was greeted by Larry, the mortician. Inside parlor A, there was Bernie who had brought bouquets of daffodils, tulips and roses…which he was placing around the casket. Jenny, who looked surprisingly elegant was making sure all the chairs were in a neat row. Both key employees came and gave Margot a big hug and escorted her to the casket.

It didn't take long for a crowd to gather even in the morning hours. Many were regular customers who Margot had met over the past several weeks. Not surprisingly, there were some folks she didn't know, but Diane and Bernie were attentive to introduce her to every greenhouse customer who attended.

By the early afternoon, Margot was amazed at size of the crowd. By 2:30, she met Frank's son, Scott, who said a few kind words and then visited the casket in private. By 6 p.m., she was absolutely flabbergasted by the large turnout, which may have totaled 100 people.

At about that time, Margot stood in front of the casket and greeted the attendees. "I want to thank you all for attending and paying your respects to Frank, who for more than four decades, ran the Westchester Greenhouse, and made it a model for all nurseries in the northeast. My name is Margot Roberts, and I am the new owner of the Greenhouse.

"I had been a long-time customer of the place for many years, and was always treated well by Frank and his loyal employees…all of whom I believe are here. When he started to get sick, he told me that he was thinking of selling the place. I was looking for a new opportunity…and the timing was right for both of us.

"I will tell you this: Frank valued his customers, suppliers and nursery friends almost as much as the plants that surrounded him every day for more than 40 years. I think he would be surprised at how many of you came this afternoon. Let me introduce his son, Scott, who came all the way from Hawaii to be here. Stand up please Scott." (He reluctantly did so). "And let me also introduce his cousin Charlie, who runs a similar greenhouse in Stamford, Connecticut. I guess it runs in the family." (his cousin stands up and salutes the audience).

After a few long breaths, Margot continued. "My, my, my. I'm a little bit of a loss for words…but I have learned that Frank is one man in a million. We will all miss him. If any of you have the flexibility, feel free to attend the church service at Sacred Heart at 9 a.m. tomorrow or the burial service right after that at Mt. Hope cemetery. Meanwhile, please share your stories with his fans here, and thank you all for coming."

With that, she looked to the audience saw many people giving her a thumbs up. Over the next several hours, she said hi to many of his fans, and met many greenhouse owners from out of state who had made the journey to be there. After paying their respects, many of them greeted Margot and said they had heard from cohorts that she ran a wonderful seminar for "Late Bloomers." Many of them wondered if she could run a similar kick-off seminar in their nurseries.

Margot shyly thanked them, but advised them that this was not the place to discuss that. Instead, she offered her card and accepted one for each inquiring However,

Finally, shortly after 9 p.m. the crowd thinned. Margot, Bernie, and Diane hugged each other and agreed to attend the church and burial the next morning.

In some ways, these were the saddest events of the ceremony.

The pastor priest, Father Anthony Meyer, said some nice words about dear Frank. Margot and the employees weren't too certain what kind of practicing Catholic Frank was, but the priest seemed to know him well enough…perhaps because of the slower winter days when he could come in late on the weekend.

The burial was even more emotional. Several dozen people formed an auto procession from the church into Mt. Hope cemetery, which was stunning in the early fall. Many of the monuments had flowers at their base, and Frank's plot was surrounded by many bouquets of flowers. In so many ways, Margot felt it was apropos to smell the fragrance of the blooms and imagine that in a bizarre way, Frank would enjoy his final resting place to be surrounded by such year round beauty.

Once the ceremony was completed, Margot and the employees hugged and slowly walked to their cars to live up to his legend, and re-open the Westchester Greenhouse.

# Chapter 30

## *Back to work.*

A**FTER A DRAMATIC PERSONAL EVENT** (SUCH AS the death of a dear friend, a funeral and a burial), many people think the best way to move forward is to simply get back to basics. That was Margot's modus operandi after laying Frank to rest in Mt. Hope cemetery.

Evidently, it was the same approach taken by Bernie and Jenny at the Westchester Greenhouse. None of them wanted to rehash the sad saga. They simply went into work and did their best to accomplish all that could be done in a day, as Frank would have urged them to do.

Fortunately, it was late fall, and there were many chores in the place before autumn flowers had a chance to blossom in the garden before the thaw hit.

After the burial, Margot had heard from several New England Greenhouse owners who had heard about her "Late Bloomers" appearances. She gratefully acknowledged their compliments, but also explained that it was time for her to get back to work. Perhaps in the spring, she gently explained…and they all urged her to call back at that time of year, and schedule something.

While the weather was still autumn warm, many people did visit the greenhouse and buy flowers that still had the chance to bloom.

In view of "the team" that Margot believed had developed at the Greenhouse, Westchester Greenhouse. Many bought forsythia bushes, which were easy to plant at this time of year, and would provide bright yellow blooms in the early spring. Others bought hardy fuschia, goldenrod, and dianthus flowers which still had a chance to bloom.

She decided to give each and everyone on staff a raise during Thanksgiving weekend. As she explained to each of them, their contributions to the Greenhouse were critical and very much appreciated by all the customers. Everyone on the staff was surprised and grateful that the extra cash has come so quickly after Margot's rise as the CEO/owner of the nursery. It would obviously come in handy during the Christmas gift-giving season.

Once things settled down, she called her dear daughter in London. Compared to Frank's son Scott, It felt great to speak with an outgoing, interested offspring.

At the beginning of the call, Margot made it all about Annie. How's the job? Got any new boyfriends? Got any trips planned? Any chance you might come to New York soon?

Most of her responses were positive. She found the job fulfilling and despite some occasional dates, still enjoyed going out with Adam. She had thought about visiting mom in New York during Christmas, but needed to check the workload at that time of year. "It might slow down and it might be possible," Anne teased, "but I really need to check the schedule. Mom, what's new with you?"

Reluctantly, Margot explained that the previous owner, Frank, had recently passed away and without any family in town, she was tasked with handling the funeral and burial.

"Yech," Anne reacted. "Sounds gruesome."

"Yeah, sort of…but there were about 100 people at the wake, and I had to give a short speech. People seem to love this nursery and felt very attached to Frank."

"As a matter of fact, I have," Margot responded.

"Mom, I am sure you did a great job, but I am sorry it was something you had to go through."

"Such is life…and death" Margot shrugged.

"Just to change the subject, do you still like the new job?" Anne asked.

"It's a great job with a great staff," Margot answered.

"By the way," Annie perked up. "Mom a few days ago, I went on Google, and looked you up. Of course, they had your transition from Citibank to the Westchester Greenhouse. But the more surprising thing is the coverage you have received for your "Late Bloomers" initiative. There's an article from the Westchester Journal. Also articles from Stamford, Boston, and Providence Rhode Island. All raves. Have you seen them?"

"I have seen most of them," Margot answered

"You should save them and get a TV interview."

"Oh, I don't know, the mom responded.

"Do you have any more planned for after the start of the year?"

"Not yet, but some other nurseries have expressed an interest."

"Save the news clippings." her daughter advised.

"I definitely will,"

After a pause, Annie said, "Mom, other than the funeral, you sound good. Are you going out with anyone?"

Margot instantly laughed. "Oh, no. I went on a few dates with a stupid senior dating site. One was a disaster. The other one was pretty good."

"So…."

"So, I got busy and never followed up on it."

"Mom, I'd try the pretty good guy again. Why not? It could be just for a few laughs. It's not like you have to move in with the guy."

"You're funny," Margot responded with a giggle.

"I learned it from my mother," she answered.

"You're too funny," Margot repeated.

After a few more minutes of chit-chat, Annie promised to check her schedule and see if a holiday trip to New York was at all possible.

"I remember from banking days, it's usually a little hectic before Christmas. Actually, it's the same rush in the nursery business….but it usually slows down between Christmas and New Year's. Check that week." mom suggested.

"I will. Meanwhile, always know, I love you," Annie answered.

"I love you back," Margot answered, and felt so lucky to have such a wonderful daughter.

# Chapter 31

## *The Holiday Plan*

A FEW DAYS LATER, ANNA CALLED BACK AND informed her mother that she would be able to come to New York the day after Christmas for one week.

"If it's OK, I might like to bring Adam," she asked. "He's never been to New York."

"Oh, that's great." Margot responded.

"Ill try to arrange some fun things to do and see. One thing for sure will be the train show at the New York Botanical Garden."

"I remember that when I was a kid," Anna said.

"It's even better now."

"And I definitely want to see the Greenhouse."

"Absolutely." Margot responded "I'll try to find a nice place to eat one night. There are more than a few in Manhattan."

"Mom, you mentioned that you went out with a pretty good guy a while back. If you want to invite him to dinner, we could have a double date." Anna teased.

"Oh, honey, I don't know...it's been a few months."

"He's probably waiting for you call," Annie kidded her mom.

"Ha, Ha. Honey, when you get your flight plans, let me know. Meanwhile, I will try to see what kind of shows there are in Manhattan."

"You're the best," Annie said.

"Thanks, babe. See you soon, Margot answered.

The Nursery was starting to get busy in anticipation of the Christmas season. When she arrived, she went to see Bernie and asked him two questions: how busy is the place over the next few weeks? Does it slow down between Christmas and New Years.

His answers did not surprise Margot.

"The ten days or two weeks before Christmas get crazy. But then it suddenly slows down quite a bit. There is still some traffic on the week after Christmas. but it's not intense. Some people come back with gift certificates and want some flowers for their visiting friends, " he answered.

"You are amazing," she answered. "And as Frank used to say, you are invaluable. By the way, does Jenny have gift certificates for people who come here Christmas shopping and don't know what to get?"

"I'm sure she has plenty, but I always try to persuade them to get an actual plant. It's more Christmassy," he answered. "You know what I should do though? We have a sound system in the greenhouse, and I should probably bring in some albums. It makes the place more festive."

"Again, you are amazing," she repeated.

That night, she looked in the newspaper to see what attractions were hot in Manhattan and Westchester in preparation for her daughter's visit. The Botanical Garden was a must see. There were a few Broadway plays that intrigued her—namely, "Some Like it Hot," and "M,J. the musical based on Michael Jackson."

What about a nice fancy restaurant in Manhattan? Using her computer google, she narrowed it down to the Union Square Restaurant, Toqueville on East 15th and the Tribeca Grill, still owned by Robert DeNiro. If she got stuck, she could always recommend a comedy show with stand-up comedians. And more locally, there were nice more casual restaurants, and beautiful views along the Hudson River.

Shortly after that, she looked in her address book and found the phone number of Wayne Philips, the man with whom she had a fairly successful date via Silver Singles. He was the guy who was originally a dentist and then had a mid-life career change into running a kennel. It was a nice date, and Margot privately wondered why she never pursued a second get-together. He had called a few times after their dinner, but Margot felt she needed to throw herself more fully into her new business. I wonder if he remembers me, she thought… but what the hell, give it a go.

She dialed his number and even wondered how the telephone conversation would go. After a few rings, there was an answer.

"Wayne," she asked.

"Yes, this is he."

"Hi, this is Margot Roberts. I don't know if you remember me, but we went on a Silver Singles date a few months ago."

"I definitely do remember you," the man answered. "I thought we had a fun time together. I even called you back a few times, but never got a response."

"I know, I'm sorry," she apologized.

"Didn't want to see me again," he teased.

"No, it wasn't that. But I do admit that this dating thing is relatively new to me."

"I know, me too," Wayne answered.

"Yeah, well, I was trying to get my new business going well. It takes work…but trouble hit. The former owner, who was schooling me on the job, got sick. In a short time, he died, so I had to handle his funeral and burial. Not fun."

"Ouch." he reacted.

"Exactly," she answered. "But I miss having some fun beyond work. And you?"

""Right. I haven't gone out with anyone after you. See, you are a tough act to follow."

"Want to give it another go?" she asked tentatively.

"I definitely do," he responded. "How about a repeat performance—another bite and cocktail at Anthony's restaurant in Elmsford?"

"Wow, you have a good memory."

"For me, it was a memorable night," he replied.

"You pick the night?"

"How about tomorrow?" he asked.

"That would be perfect. Do you remember where I live? "

"I do. And it's casual. I'll keep the dogs at home," he kidded her.

"Probably a good idea."

"7:30.?" he asked.

"Sounds good. See you then." Margot answered and then hung up.

In fact, Wayne did sound good. For the first time in many weeks, Margot did look forward to a meal with a friend.

# CHAPTER 32

## *The host of NYC.*

MARGOT'S DATE WITH WAYNE WAS BETTER AND more effortless than the one she had months ago with him. She even had a few laughs. That was particularly welcomed, especially after the tough days of Frank's burial.

She asked him if it was a busy time of year for him.

"Yeah, a little bit," he confessed. "I have a lot of dogs in the kennel and at this time of year, many people think it would be a good time to give a puppy to a dear friend, neighbor, or family member."

"Do they pick out the dog ahead of time," she asked.

"Definitely. I usually put a reserved tag around their neck so I know it's spoken for," he answered.

"When do they come to pick up the pup?" she wondered.

actually a bunch of fun. So I'll be making plans. I'll give you a call and tell you which

"Usually Christmas eve day," he responded. "Sometimes, Christmas day. I keep the place open just in case the buyers want to make it a living, breathing, barking Christmas surprise."

"Does it slow down after that?" she wondered.

"It usually does."

"That's what I told my daughter who is coming in town to visit me from London between Christmas and New Year's."

"It's still a great festive time of year," he acknowledged.

"Yeah, I was thinking of having a nice NYC dinner with her and her boyfriend. I was wondering if you'd care to join us."

"Sounds fun."

"I'm sure you could make it so. By the way, my dear daughter Annie is wonderful daughter, who wants the dates of her visit to to be good for all of us….but it will definitely be a few days after Christmas. I'll need the time at the nursery for folks who want to cash in their gift certificates."

"How's it going there?" Wayne asked.

"It's good. This is the crazy time of year, but I have a great staff…and I have a hunch January and February will be dead."

"I would think so."

That was the way their conversation went on their next date. Easy as pie. As a matter of fact, Wayne asked if she wanted a nightcap after dinner, and Margot agreed with a smile.

She simply agreed to another glass of wine. They clinked glasses and shared a few more laughs. When he brought her home, she gave him a kiss on the lips, and looked forward to being with him again.

It would be several weeks. At this time of year, she had to give the Greenhouse full days—including early mornings and sometimes a few hours after closing.

It would be almost as busy as May, June, July, and August. Of course, the offerings were different than in the summer. However, the spirit in the place was infectious. She was thankful that she had such a good staff who could help the customers find just the right flowers and plants, and even help them bring their new purchases to their car.

The music supplied by Bernie on the sound system was perfect for the season. No big rap or hip-hop….just classics from Sinatra, Bing Crosby, Michael Buble, Cindy Lauper, and Eartha Kitt. Margot's favorites was "It's beginning to look a lot like Christmas" and "Here Comes Santa Clause." She definitely liked the tempo and believed they helped put the customers in a happy, buying mood.

Taking a cue from Wayne, she decided to keep the place open on Christmas Day so her customers could get the fragrant gifts they had pre-ordered. In deference to her staff, she decided that the Christmas hours should be from noon-six, so they and their family could open up gifts on Christmas morning. They all appreciated the morning off so they could hug their families and loved ones.

As scheduled with her daughter, Annie and Adam arrived on Friday, the 27th of December. Given the length of the flight, Margot had prepared a home cooked meal, so everyone could relax and get a good night sleep before a busy tourista week.

On Saturday, the two kids took the car up to Kingston, New York, where they boarded the Polar Express train ride. Once inside the holiday train, the dancing chefs make the trip to "the North Pole," where they met Santa, who leads everyone in Christmas Carols. Margot had explained that she would need to work at the Greenhouse on both weekend days, but truly invited them to have fun on their own.

On Sunday, she had purchased an Uber gift certificate and a Broadway matinee ticket for MJ, the musical for Anna and Adam in Manhattan. Back home, Anna and Adam raved about the fun they had, and hoped Margot could join them for a few days.

On Monday, all three of them went to the New York Botanical Garden and saw the miniature train display in the Haupt Conservatory.

On Tuesday, both Annie and Adam wanted to visit Times Square and watch the ball fall for a memorable New Year's eve. Annie tried to persuade her mother to visit with them, but Margot had no desire to be there with the crazy crowd. She suggested that the two kids visit the Whitney during the day to see the Edward Hopper exhibit and then head to the New Year's Eve countdown. Just so they could get home safely, she gave them another Uber gift pass in and out of Manhattan.

Wednesday, Margot had scheduled a meal in lower Manhattan with her friend Graham, who picked them up in Westchester and drove the foursome to the Tribeca Grill, which is owned by Robert DeNiro, who wasn't there that evening. So what? Annie, Adam. Margot and Graham had a great meal and lots of laughs. Annie particularly got a kick out of Graham, and after he dropped them all off at Margot's house, encouraged her mom to enjoy the man on a more regular basis.

On Thursday, the young folks went to nearby Lyndhurst to see this historic sight once owned by Jay Gould, and was now adorned with Christmas lights on the lawn, the trees, and inside the house.

Of course, all good things must come to an end. Friday was Annie and Adam"s flight back to London. Over lunch with mom, they reviewed the week and thanked the mom for all she had done to make their stay in New York so memorable. The two young folks hoped she could come to London again sometime soon. Margot promised she would take a look at her schedule, but admitted she had a big year ahead of her, including several "Late Bloomer" presentations.

"Please try," Annie pleaded and gave her mom a kiss. She then greeted the limo in the driveway, and made sure all the bags were secure in the trunk. As the big black Lincoln pulled away, Margot waved goodbye to the young couple and slowly watched the car pull away down the street. It was sad to see the limo disappear, but she did have to admit it was damn fun to feel the sense of a family.

# Chapter 33

## *Winter in the Greenhouse.*

A s she had anticipated, January and February were deadly months in the northern Westchester nursery business. Some days, there were only a few dozen people who visited the greenhouse.

Margot looked at her balance sheet, and saw that many of the staff members used the slow season to take a vacation in the sun. She asked Jenny if she was planning to go South during the month.

"I'd like to visit some of my relatives in New Orleans," she responded.

"You should do it. I'm sure Bernie can handle the cash register." When she asked Bernie, he gladly agreed, and suggested that he take a week in Florida, as soon as Jenny got back.

Meanwhile, Margot quizzed the staff and addressed the winter vacation

"Find it. And chase the sunshine for a few days," Bernie encouraged.

"You are a champ," Margot answered and patted him on the back. question. Most of them did, in fact, plan to take at least a week off during the cold, winter season….and admitted they had done so for many years, when Frank was in charge.

When Bernie came back and got in the swing of things, he even suggested that Margot take some time away from the snow in the

Northeast. "Why not go to Florida for a few days. You've earned it," he complimented her.

"I might," she nodded. "At the funeral, a greenhouse owner from St. Pete Beach wanted me to give my presentation on "Late Bloomers," but I told him that the wake was not the time to discuss it. "I think I have his card somewhere."

Overhearing the conversation, Jenny joined in. "Margot, you could combine a trip to Florida with a trip to Louisiana. My cousin owns a greenhouse down there, and I told him about your successes up here. He encouraged me to talk to you about making a trip down to New Orleans. I have his number. Ever been to New Orleans?"

"Nope," Margot answered.

"Well, it's a fun place."

"And so is St.Pete Beach," Bernie argued.

That night, there was a 4" snowstorm in Westchester County, and Margot considered the kind advice of her two most valuable workers.

For starters, she called the man from Florida. His name was Bennie Calhoun, and he was a nephew of Frank, and had attended the funeral in New York. He was also a relative of Charlie Claggett, the greenhouse owner in Stamford Connecticut, and had heard of the success of Margot's seminars.

That was perhaps why he introduced himself to the woman at the funeral and gave her his card.

"Mr. Calhoun," she began her phone conversation. "My name is Margot Roberts, and I am now the owner of the Westchester Greenhouse in New York. I believe I met you at Frank's funeral before Thanksgiving. Do you remember me?"

"I do," Bennie answered. "By the way, you gave a wonderful address at my uncle Frank's service."

"Thanks,"

"And I had heard from him that you were a true wiz in the nursery, and had begun a program that celebrated his most regular customers. Evidently, it gained a lot of publicity for the nursery and increased sales a lot. He wanted me to talk to you."

"Well, I have given the one-day seminar in several states now, and it seems to reward regular customers ….and Greenhouse owners.

"What's it called?" Bennie asked.

"Late Bloomers." she answered. "It speaks to customers who have gone through a mid-life career change."

"Omigod, I have dozens of them here in Florida. Can you come down here and talk to them?"

"I would love to do so next month when it's frigid in New York."

"Come down here and bring a bathing suit." he chuckled.

`Throughout the rest of the conversation, she scheduled a date, and requested that Bennie invite his 15 best mid-life career changing customers. She also suggested that they invite a photographer and writer from his local newspaper. As she explained, the seminar seems to make a good story, and build good publicity for his greenhouse.

"Consider it done," Bennie said, and they agreed to keep in touch over the next few days.

After that conversation, she spoke with Harry Wilkins, the cousin and greenhouse owner of Jenny, who had prepped the call and the pitch. When Margot called, Harry was expecting her pitch. In fact, Jenny had built up the success of the one-day seminar so much, he was hoping she would call. By and large, it was a successful as her call to Bennie in Florida. Looking at her calendar, she scheduled it a few days after the St. Pete meeting, so she would have time to get from one Southern city to the next.

At the end of both calls, she opened the door and looked at the Northeastern snowstorm blanketing the yard and the streets. Given her shivers, it made her feel good that she had scheduled two seminars for the warm southern climate.

# CHAPTER 34

# *Margot's message spreads south.*

After talking with Cliff about her upcoming seminars, Margot ordered 30 more prints of "Late Bloomers," "Gladly," Cliff responded. "The publicity has been a godsend for me. As a matter of fact, I have been awarded a solo art show in Tampa, Florida."

"Hooray for you," Margot answered. "Is that close to St. Petersburg Beach?"

"I think it's about a 30 minute drive"

"Amazing. I have a seminar in St. Pete Beach the last week in February."

"I'll be in Tampa for the show…but can I attend your session?"

"It would be my thrill." she answered. "As usual, it will be at the end of the nursery day. And there will be news folks there. It'll be good for you, good for the Greenhouse, and good for me."

"Perfect," he answered.

When the meeting date arrived, Bennie kicked off the meeting by thanking all of his valuable customers for attending. He explained that his cousin in New York told him about this movement and this woman, Margot.

He then pointed to a table which contained 15 Celosia plants which were due to bloom in the next few weeks. "These are late bloomers which are rare in Florida," he said. But they will bring you new fragrance and beauty in the next few weeks. And speaking of late bloomers, it's also an apt description of every one of you. I understand that many of you are thinking of career changes....or have already started new careers in the past few year. That's Margot's story too. And I will now turn it over to her to explain the connection with Celosia plants."

There was some gentle applause for Bennie, who gave the center stage to Margot. There were also some photos from the news media.

"Hello, everyone. I am so tickled to be here," she began. "Bennie has been so nice to me during my stay here in Florida. He may have stolen some of my thunder, but let me get a little more specific."

"I was a banker for more than 30 years, and always loved going to greenhouse. It helped me feel revived. Fresh again, New again. Reborn.

Rejuvenated. As you know, you can feel that way just walking through this greenhouse.

"But I never felt it after 3 decades in the bank. And then I got the opportunity of a lifetime...to recreate my life, and buy that greenhouse. Thanks to that, I feel alive every day....but I am not alone.

"One of my dear friends....Cliff, please stand up....he underwent the same transition. After many decades as a business executive, he decided to follow his passion and become a fine artist. He now has a solo show in Tampa.

"I brought a print of his piece for each of you. It celebrates so many people who have made the same choice—to reinvent their careers in mid-life.

After the next day in the sun, Margot headed off to New Orleans, which astonished her as a surprisingly vibrant city.

At the nursery, she repeated her appeal to reinvigorate one's life like an ever-blooming flower and handed out late-bloomer prints to all the attendees who had been hand-picked by the owner as valuable customers who had changed careers in mid-life. Many of the names in this piece of art are late bloomers like yourself, and it's illustrated with a lilac blooming in the snow.

"You all should get one, and keep coming to this nursery to feel regenerated. Meanwhile, I wish you all the best in your new lives. Questions? Comments?"

As usual, there were many comments from the attendees. Some admitted the struggle of the mid-life career change. Others proudly explained their new lives. During this, the newsman and photographer took pictures of many of the attendees…and Bennie, Margot and Cliff.

The news people from the New Orleans Times-Picayune were impressed by the topic. They quizzed many of the attendees about their fears in making a mid-life career change. They wondered about the adjustment period in a new occupation. They asked if any of them had been tempted to go back to their original jobs. The answer: none.

Afterwards, they did interview Margot for about 20 minutes. They asked her how long it she considered her transition from banking to horticulture. Answer: a few years. They congratulated her on her initiative, and spreading it in many American cities.

At the end of the day, she felt revived about the day. The next morning, she enjoyed her day in the sun before heading off to New Orleans.. That evening, she visited downtown New Orleans with Jenny and thoroughly enjoyed it. Her greenhouse address was covered by the New Orleans Times-Picayune. Once again, it was a rave. The next morning, she prepared for a three and half hour flight back to New York. However, she proudly admitted to herself that the trip was well worth it.

# CHAPTER 35

## *The News Spreads.*

WITHIN TWO WEEKS, THE GREENHOUSE OWNERS IN St. Pete Beach and New Orleans did send the news articles to Margot, along with effusive thanks for running the seminar. They also acknowledged that their sales had skyrocketed after the news articles hit the news stands.

The St. Pete Beach News gave the event a two column article in the local events section. It explained the gist of the afternoon meeting and featured a photo of Margot , Bennie and Cliff the artist.

The article in the New Orleans Times Picayune was even more effusive. It ran on page 2 of the popular newspaper and was three columns long. It applauded the efforts of Ms. Margot Roberts of Westchester county, New York who "initiated a movement in many U.S, greenhouses to applaud late bloomers, which she explains is not just flowers…but human beings who endeavor to recreate their lives in their 30's, 40's, 50's and beyond."

There was an accompanying editorial, which called the endeavor "not just timely in a post-covid world, but also downright inspirational. "

"Wow." Margot silently uttered as she read the articles.

As usual, she did not brag about the articles to her own employees at the Westchester Greenhouse. However, it did feel good to be back in the flower business with a fresh tan from the deep South.

She did thank Bernie and Jenny for the leads to their nursery friends in Florida and New Orleans. Both of them said that their friends in the south had forwarded the news articles.

"Very impressive," Bernie said.

"I was blown away by the publicity…as were all my long lost friends in New Orleans," Jenny added.

"Again, thank you, thank you,:" Margot replied. "But it's nice to be back at work, especially with two of my favorite people."

In the weeks ahead, she and the staff began to prepare for the spring season. It would mean a deep clean of all the aisles, an increase in vegetable plants, and many displays of early blooming flowers, Also, at this time of year, the customers began to increase. Most of them were familiar faces, and it was good to see them after the long, cold winter.

Two visitors did not fit in that stereotype. One was named Randall Cameron, who explained that he was a writer for the New York Times. The other was Rachel Jackson, a photographer for the same publication.

Randall did most of the talking. When he gave her his card, he explained the purpose of their visit to Margot. "Perhaps you know that the New York Times covers news stories from all over the United States.

"And the world," Rachel added.

"Yes," Randall agreed. "But when we look at the news stories across the nation, we are particularly drawn to stories about New York citizens."

"Not necessarily NYC residents. They can be residents of Westchester County or anywhere in the New York area."

"Thank you Rachel," Randall answered with the slightest sarcasm in his voice.

"Lately, we have noticed many stories about you and your greenhouse in news stories from Westchester to Providence to Stamford, to Tampa, to New Orleans."

"Those greenhouse owners have been very generous in inviting me and making sure that there was news coverage.," Margot acknowledged.

"Well, it looks like they have all succeeded," he replied. "And we would like to feature you and your message in America's number one newspaper."

"With pictures," Rachel added.

"With pictures," Randall repeated.

"Wow." Margot responded. "What exactly would you like to know?"

Randall was a pro at interviewing people. He asked is she had a good 45-minutes for an in-depth interview.

Given the slow time of the year, Margot responded yes.

The reporter went through her full story—from her years at Citibank, her wanuderlust after many decades, to her purchase of the greenhouse. She covered the funeral of Frank. And she also gave a full account in her happiness there, and her endeavors to cover "Late Bloomers" in so many U.S. cities.

"Can we get a picture of painting on your wall?" Rachel, the photographer asked.

"Of course,"

"Can we get pictures of your greenhouse with some of your key staff members?" Randall asked.

"Definitely," she answered emphatically.

In a short time, she asked Bernie and Jenny to join her in a photo in several photos—one in front of the plants, one in front of the entrance sign, one in front of the shrubs and trees.

When the interview was done, Margot thanked the Times staff for visiting, and offered her card if they had any further questions.

"By the way, it's a beautiful greenhouse," Rachel added as a final thought.

"Thank you. Thank you very much," she answered and walked them back to their car.

Afterwards, in a rare treat, Margot poured a glass of Rose from her office fridge and poured a glass for Bernie and Jenny. She toasted them.

"I hope you could know how very much I value you…and the rest of the staff," she said.

"We do," Bernie answered.

"And we are so glad to have you here as the head of the greenhouse." Rachel added.

After a sip, Bernie asked, "Do you think it will be a positive article?"

"Yes," Margot responded. "And I predict we will have an unusually busy spring season."

# CHAPTER 36

# *The NY Times makes her famous.*

THE NEW YORK TIMES ARTICLE CREATED QUITE a buzz. People came to the Westchester Greenhouse and asked specifically to speak with Margot. They all shook her hand and congratulated her on newspaper raves.

The actual article explained her mid-life mission in life and referenced the stories that had been published in six American cities. As their news story reported, "We seem to have a breakthrough visionary in our midst who inspires people everywhere she speaks."

"It's an extremely relevant encouragement, since people 18-24 change jobs 5.7 times, compared with workers 45-52 who change careers only 1.9 times. Of course, it's not all about money. Most people seek a career change because their philosophy and goals have changed. Many people find the leadership at the current job is not to their liking.

As Margot continued reading the article, she proudly smiled. As she did so, the telephone began to ring.

"Hello," she answered.

"Mom, this is your dear daughter. Did you read the recent article about you in the New York Times?

As a matter of fact, I was just reading it now. Pretty flattering, I must admit."

"That's putting it mildly," Annie retorted. "It basically describes you as a genius. And thanks to my advanced Google search keys,

I also read the stories in the Florida and New Orleans papers. All good…but the Times article is the capper. That paper is read in every city in America, and most locales around the world."

"You are too sweet," Margot said. company is unsatisfactory. Even more want a better work-life balance.

"The encouragement that Margot gives to the 50 plus crowd is a godsend. It's not just the young folks that have ambition, as any mid-life person can tell you."

"I showed it to Adam too," Annie said. "He was absolutely staggered by how glowingly they wrote about you."

'Thank him too."

"Mom, I am so proud of you…but I have to get back to work. I just wanted to call and make sure you had the chance to read the raves. Love you, mom."

"Love you back." Margot answered and said goodbye. Then she walked around the house, smelling the roses, and viewing the "Late Bloomers" artwork in her dining room.

While she was doing this, the phone rang again. "Is this Margot the celebrity?" the man asked.

Recognizing his voice, she countered, "Is this Graham, the successful animal lover and kennel owner?"

"Indeed it is, but I don't get in the New York Times for that. However, you my dear, are described as a superstar!"

"You liked the article?" she coyly asked.

"Are you kidding me? It's bravissimo! Let's go out an celebrate!"

"Where?"

"I don't care. Someplace nice. Maybe Xavier's on the Hudson," he said.

"I've never been there, but I hear it's nice." She responded.

"It will be all the nicer with you. Can I pick you up in an hour?" Graham asked.

"If you'd like to."

"I'd love to," he answered and dressed up for the evening.

An hour later, Graham rang Margot's doorbell and gave her a kiss and a hug when she answered. On the way to Xavier's, she discussed her reaction to the news article, and how thrilled she was that her daughter called her all the way from London.

"She's a nice and beautiful girl," he said.

"And she thinks the world of you," Margot responded.

"Now I like her even more," Graham kidded.

Over dinner, they toasted each other, and had some laughs. Margot had to admit to herself she enjoyed being with Graham. He was a nice looking man about her same age. And it had been a long time since he felt so at ease with a person of the opposite sex.

As was his habit, they had a nightcap toast, and then under the moon, headed back to her home town. Once they arrived, he walked her to the door, and she gave him a kiss on the lips with a tight hug. Before he left, he gave her a look in the eye, and returned the favor of sweet kiss.

Then the idea occurred to her….for the first time in perhaps six years. "Would you like to join me inside?" she asked as sexily as she could remember.

"If you'd like to have me," he answered.

"I think I would very much like to have you," she said.

One thing led to another. A hug. Another kiss. Another hug.

Graham asked if he could use her phone. He dialed his number at the kennel. "Bruce are you there? Can you handle something for me tonight? I'm tied up with a friend, and I'd like you to feed all the dogs and give them a walk first thing in the morning. Great! You're the best, Bruce," he said and hung up.

Within seconds, the couple rejoined the hugs and kisses. Within minutes, they went to bedroom and took that passion to the big King sized bed. At this point, there was not a lot of talk. Both knew the next move, It had been a long time for both of them, but it all came back.

At sunrise, both were smiling and Margot made coffee for Graham. He enjoyed it and explained that he really did have to get back to the kennel, but thoroughly enjoyed the evening.

She nodded and gave him a morning kiss and hug as he headed for the door.

While in the doorway, she blew him a kiss and waved good-bye…for now.

All morning at the greenhouse, she was giggling. He was doing the same thing at the kennel.

# CHAPTER 37

# *Morning Joe.*

ONCE SHE GOT TO THE GREENHOUSE, SHE retrieved two phone messages from a man named John Kelly, a producer for the "Morning Joe" television show. Never one to ignore messages, she called the man on the 212 number which he left for her.

"Mr. Kelly," she began. "My name is Margot Roberts, and it looks like you have been trying to reach me."

"Indeed I have been, " he answered. "I have been following some of the news stories about you…and I recently shared them with Mika and Joe. They both thought it was a very relevant topic for the times."

"Thank you very much," she responded. "Once I recreated my life in the nursery business, I began running some after-hours groups on the subject of re-inventing your life in mid-career. To be honest, I was partly inspired by the plants in my greenhouse that were rejuvenation year after year…after year."

"Exactly," John answered. "You sound as if you can easily talk about the subject, which could be a big plus on television.

"Thank you," Margot said.

"The reason that may be important is that Mika thought it would be a good topic to showcase on the show, and Joe definitely agreed. Do you ever watch the show?"

"As a matter of fact I do…every morning before heading to the greenhouse."

"Here's the key question for you," John continued. "Would you have any interest in appearing on the show for a ten-minute segment?"

"Omigod, I've never even thought of the possibility," she answered with some surprise in her voice.

""When do you think you could do it?" John Kelly asked.

"You tell me," she responded.

"Let's make it next Tuesday," he said. "You probably need to be there at 6:30 a.m. to prepare for the 7:30 segment. But I'll call you on Monday before just to reconfirm and answer any questions you might have before the show."

"Sounds great," she replied. "I look forward to it."

"That's what many first-timers say," he replied. "But you sound self-assured on the phone. And bear in mind, you would not be doing all the talking. If you watch the show, you know that Mika and Joe like to talk a lot…and they usually have some guests on the panel, who would also open their mouths. Whadya say?"

After a few second pause, Margot replied. "I guess it might be worth a try."

"That's great. I think you would be excellent on the show…and the TV audience would undoubtedly like it, and gain some insights for their own lives."

"I look forward to it."

"Thanks. See you then," john answered and then said goodbye.

On the Tuesday, Margot got up early and drove to 30 Rockefeller Center, where "Morning Joe" is filmed. She dressed up spiffy, brought a potted plant of gardenias, and a print of "Late Bloomers." As she had promised John Kelly, she arrived at the studio at 6:30 a.m.

There were a few other people there—Claire McCaskill, the former Senator, Donny Deutsch, who podcasts Brand Up, Brand Down, and a make-up artist—who offered to help make all the folks ready for the camera. Donny refused, but Claire and Margot gladly took advantage of the make-up artist's expertise.

Before long, it was 7:20, and John Kelly came into the green room and asked if everyone was ready. Hearing the affirmative, he escorted them all down the hall to the studio. "They have switched to a weather forecast for about 5 minutes including commercials, "John explained. "It's a good time to take your seats around the "Morning Joe" table.

As semi-regulars on the show, Claire and Donny knew where to go. When Margot entered the room, Mika and Joe rose to shake her hands and show her where to sit—right next to Mika. While they waited for airtime, Mika told Margot that she was excited to meet her. Joe added that they had read many newx articles about her.

Once settled, a staff member came to table and gave Joe, Mika, and every guest a fresh glass of ice water, and then quickly escaped. As he did so, Margot could hear the sound in the background of a countdown: 5-4-3-then a silent 2 and 1.

"Welcome back to 'Morning Joe' Mika announced and then pointed to the table. We have some good guests here for this segment—Hello Claire McCaskill, Hello Donny Deutchs....and hello and welcome to a special guest named Margot Roberts, the owner of the Westchester Greenhouse (hence the potted plant which she brought to the show). However, she wasn't always a gardener.. In fact, she was a banker for more than 30 years, before making a big career change and founding "Late Bloomers"—which celebrates people who decide in mid-life to chase another dream. Welcome to the show, Margot."

"Thanks for inviting me," Margot said.

"So tell us," Joe jumped in. "You hated banking and it took 30 years to realize that?"

The table laughed, and Margot answered. "I didn't really hate banking. In fact, I believe I helped many people get their home loans, save for their kid's college education, and maybe even transition to a new career. But I sat in the same desk everyday, and enjoyed going to the local greenhouse. I also took lots of classes at the New York Botanical Garden, where I discovered how refreshing it can be to be around plants and shrubs. The previous owner wanted to find a way out. One thing led to another, and before long, I left life in a bank… and became the new owner. My message is: it's never too late."

Mika chimed in. "I often tell that to women who dream of success.. It's a long runway."

"Good advice," Margot nodded in agreement.

"It's true," Claire McCaskill added her two-cents worth. "I'm a good case in point, I was in the U.S. Senate for 12 years until 2019. And very much in my mid-life. In my case, the voters decided my fate. After winning many elections, they said "enough." So what should I do? Sit in a corner and cry? No, partly thanks to "Morning Joe," I became a news analyst for NBC and MSNBC. It's more fun than sitting in a senate seat."

"And I have found my job more fun than banking, "Margot agreed. So I started this movement called "Late Bloomers." I began it at my own nursery, but by now, I have given the seminar at 7 other nurseries in 7 different states. I invite regular customers who are undergoing that mid-life point—either with a new job or thinking of a new job. You know, Americans from 18-29 change their jobs every couple years….but once you get over 50, people only change jobs once until retirement. By then, I think they are afraid of change. But what I have found is that change is good. Take a look at this Gardenia I took from the nursery. If you keep it in the dark, it will just stagnate. Give it some light, and it will become a late bloomer."

"I love that. Let me jump in," Joe smiled and began his life lesson. "As most of you know, I started as a lawyer and then went to congress. I served for 7 years…but something in my tummy told me that change could be good for me. Revitalizing like this plant. Refreshing like the flowers in a nursery. So I said goodbye to the same, old, same old…and went into broadcasting. A good move on my part."

"My history is somewhat similar.," Donny Deutsch interjected. "I ran a big successful ad agency for many decades. I was the CEO and owner of the place…but as some people know, advertising is a young person's game. Eventually, I got a very profitable offer. I was over 50, and decided there were better things to do in life than sit under an umbrella on a topical island. So I restarted my life in 2004. I formed a thing called "Brand Up, Brand Down." It's a podcast and fortunately, I get plenty of air time. "Brand up, Brand down" he repeated. "And you, Margot Roberts are definitely "Brand Up.""

"Wow, thank you, Donny," Margot responded. "And Mika and Joe…I brought a present for you. It's a piece of artwork called "Late Bloomers." As you can see, it's a list of many people who became famous and productive after their 20's, 30's, 40's, 50's and 60's. The artwork is a orchid blooming in the snow. I am proud of it, since I helped convince a man in his 50's to move beyond a successful car dealerhip and devote himself to art—his true passion. His name is Cliff Sanders and he now has gallery shows all over."

Mika looked at the art print and couldn't help but gush. "I love it."

"I do too." Joe added. "We should hang it in the house and let the kids study it, so they don't think it's all over and out in their early 20's."

"Margot, you are a miracle," Mika said. "Have you ever heard of my foundation of '50 over 50." It's a celebration of women who make their mark in the world over the age of 50. It's too late for this year, but you should consider it for next year. You can recommend yourself, or have someone recommend you. I've got a hunch you have dozens of people who would be glad to write something good about you."

"Oh, that's so nice," Margot blushed.

"That's Margot Roberts, the founder of "Late Bloomers," Mika summed up the interview.

"It's a good, worthy cause," Joe joined in. "Margot, it was a real pleasure to have you on the show."

Within a few seconds, John came on the set and told Margot it was time to leave during the commercial break. She had 2 and half minutes to get out of the studio, which was no big rush.

Once outside, John congratulated her. "Margot, that was spectacular. I am sure they will have lots of positive feedback from the session."

"I hope so. To my surprise, I actually enjoyed it, and felt comfortable." she answered.

"Keep in touch," he advised her.

"I definitely will,' she answered and thanked him for the opportunity.

Once she got to the nursery, Bernie greeted her with a smile and a hug.

"I watched the show," he acknowledged. "You were terrific! And I would be glad to write a recommendation for the 'Know Your Value' 50 over 50 event."

"That's so nice of you," she answered.

"It would be my pleasure."

About 30 minutes later, she got a call from Graham. "Bravissimo," he said, using one of his favorite words. "Let's go out and have fun again tonight. I'll pick the place. Unless you are too tired from your big show, I'll find a nice place to celebrate your new fame."

"I would love to be with you tonight, Graham," she answered.

"I'll pick you up at 7 p.m," he suggested.

As happened last time, he called Bruce when he escorted Margot into her house. "Bruce, please walk the dogs and give them food. I'm having a big, beautiful night."

Consequently, the night was indeed beautiful—for both Graham and Margot.

The next morning, she received a call from Annie. "Mom, thanks to Google, I saw you on "Morning Joe," You were spectacular—every bit as good as everyone on the panel. New thought for you: you should write a book on the topic and be a regular on the show next year. And I want to see you on the "50 over 50" spectacular next year. Gotta go…I am at work."

After hanging up, Margot walked around the house for some time just to gather her thoughts. She looked at that painting by Cliff and was thankful for the role he played in his success. She watered the many plants in the living room and dining room and filled her lungs with the sweet aroma. She reflected on the progress she had made over the past year. Given the popularity of her seminars, she even considered which locales might be next. Los Angeles? Santa Fe? Michigan? Missouri?

Ahh, where to begin? Thanks to her daughter, she had a good clue, and that brought on a smile.

Ahh, first things first. She turned on her computer, brought out clean white printer papers, and started writing the book tentatively called "Late Bloomers" that very night.

www.ingramcontent.com/pod-product-compliance
Lightning Source LLC
Chambersburg PA
CBHW020117310726
48970CB00002B/678

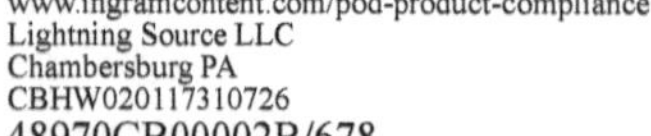